THE BLACKSMITH'S DAUGHTER

Tilly Masters hopes to follow in her father's footsteps as the village blacksmith and is upset when he takes on an assistant. But she falls in love with Nathan and is devastated when he enlists and is sent to France. She vows to wait for him but her aunt has other ambitions for her — marriage to the local squire's son. Will Tilly succumb to his advances or cling to the hope that Nathan will return from the war?

ROBERTA GRIEVE

◆

THE BLACKSMITH'S DAUGHTER

Complete and Unabridged

LINFORD
Leicester

First published in Great Britain in 2010

First Linford Edition
published 2011

Copyright © 2010 by Roberta Grieve

British Library CIP Data

Grieve, Roberta.
 The blacksmith's daughter. - -
 (Linford romance library)
 1. Blacksmiths- -Fiction. 2. Recruiting and
 enlistment- -Fiction. 3. Love stories.
 4. Large type books.
 I. Title II. Series
 823.9'2–dc22

 ISBN 978–1–44480–566–6

Published by
F. A. Thorpe (Publishing)
Anstey, Leicestershire

Set by Words & Graphics Ltd.
Anstey, Leicestershire
Printed and bound in Great Britain by
T. J. International Ltd., Padstow, Cornwall

and took a de
any business c
you'll find my
with things as

Tilly brush
away from he
smudge across
her father's de
like working v
to get this
Farmer Johns
home from m:

'Well, it's no

'Did you co
me you don't
my daughter?'

'No, I want
with you.' She
too busy at th
cottage.' She
you can find
aunt a cup of
from town.' SI

Ben had sta
the plough sl
done, lass. Be

1

Audible even over the sound of the hammer striking white-hot iron, the voice rang out, 'What on earth are you up to, girl?'

Startled, Tilly Masters let go of the bellows handle and turned to face the tall, thin woman dressed all in black who stood in the doorway of the smithy, hands on her hips, glaring.

Tilly thought she might be a potential customer so she bit back the hasty retort which sprang to her lips. She was glad she had when she realised it was her Aunt Ada whom she hadn't seen since her mother's funeral three years ago. No wonder she hadn't recognised her, although there was a slight resemblance. The difference was, Rose Masters had always been smiling, the lines at the corners of her eyes from laughter, not frowns. The woman in

1

front of her loo
time since she'

Before Tilly
nodded grimly
heard were t
accusing finger.
of, Ben Master
do the work of

Ben didn't lo
shaping the plo
tongs. He gave
hammer and p
ment into the
nodding to Til
bellows. Only
stony-faced wo

'Well, Ada B
to Lydford? C
usual, eh?'

'I came to s
my niece.' Her
the smithy. 'A
from well. Wha
say if she were
this poor girl?'

Ben clenche

see what she wants. I'll be in as soon as I can.'

Tilly didn't want to face her aunt. She seemed the sort of woman who would find fault whatever you did — just like some of their customers. Well, she was used to dealing with them and had found a way of talking to them that usually sent them on their way with a smile. Surely she could win Aunt Ada round as well.

She took off the leather apron she wore to protect her skirt from flying sparks and went outside, pausing to breathe in the cool autumn air, so refreshing after the heat of the smithy. Reluctantly she entered the cottage that adjoined the forge, glancing round the cosy sitting room to make sure nothing was out of place. Her aunt seemed the sort of person whose eye would settle on the smallest speck of dust, a cushion unplumped or an ornament a fraction out of place.

Ada was at the kitchen range, pouring water into the teapot. She had

1

Audible even over the sound of the hammer striking white-hot iron, the voice rang out, 'What on earth are you up to, girl?'

Startled, Tilly Masters let go of the bellows handle and turned to face the tall, thin woman dressed all in black who stood in the doorway of the smithy, hands on her hips, glaring.

Tilly thought she might be a potential customer so she bit back the hasty retort which sprang to her lips. She was glad she had when she realised it was her Aunt Ada whom she hadn't seen since her mother's funeral three years ago. No wonder she hadn't recognised her, although there was a slight resemblance. The difference was, Rose Masters had always been smiling, the lines at the corners of her eyes from laughter, not frowns. The woman in front of her looked as if it was a long time since she'd last smiled.

Before Tilly could speak, the woman nodded grimly. 'So, the rumours I heard were true.' She pointed an accusing finger. 'What are you thinking of, Ben Masters, letting your daughter do the work of a man?'

Ben didn't look up, concentrating on shaping the plough blade he held in the tongs. He gave a final blow with the hammer and plunged the iron implement into the water tank to cool, nodding to Tilly to stop pumping the bellows. Only then did he address the stony-faced woman.

'Well, Ada Bradford, what brings you to Lydford? Come to cause trouble as usual, eh?'

'I came to see that all was well with my niece.' Her steely gaze swept round the smithy. 'And I see that all is far from well. What would her poor mother say if she were here to see how you treat this poor girl?'

Ben clenched his fist on the hammer

and took a deep breath. 'Not that it's any business of yours, Ada, but I think you'll find my daughter is quite happy with things as they are.'

Tilly brushed a stray lock of hair away from her face, leaving a black smudge across her cheek and leapt to her father's defence. 'Yes, I am happy. I like working with Pa. Besides, he's got to get this harrow mended before Farmer Johnson calls in on his way home from market.'

'Well, it's not right, that's all.'

'Did you come all this way just to tell me you don't approve of the way I treat my daughter?' Ben asked.

'No, I wanted to discuss something with you.' She sniffed. 'I can see you're too busy at the moment. I'll wait in the cottage.' She turned to Tilly. 'Maybe you can find time to make your old aunt a cup of tea. It's a long drive out from town.' She walked away.

Ben had started to smooth and polish the plough share. 'I've got to get this done, lass. Better get in the house and see what she wants. I'll be in as soon as I can.'

Tilly didn't want to face her aunt. She seemed the sort of woman who would find fault whatever you did — just like some of their customers. Well, she was used to dealing with them and had found a way of talking to them that usually sent them on their way with a smile. Surely she could win Aunt Ada round as well.

She took off the leather apron she wore to protect her skirt from flying sparks and went outside, pausing to breathe in the cool autumn air, so refreshing after the heat of the smithy. Reluctantly she entered the cottage that adjoined the forge, glancing round the cosy sitting room to make sure nothing was out of place. Her aunt seemed the sort of person whose eye would settle on the smallest speck of dust, a cushion unplumped or an ornament a fraction out of place.

Ada was at the kitchen range, pouring water into the teapot. She had already set out the best cups and saucers on the scrubbed kitchen table. 'Look at the state of you, girl,' she said as Tilly came in. 'That's man's work your father's making you do,' she said, not hiding her disapproval.

Tilly went and washed her hands under the pump over the stone sink in the corner. 'He doesn't make me — I want to do it. You don't understand, Aunt. Nobody does.'

She sighed. 'I wish I could explain the feeling I get when I make something. It's just an ugly old lump of iron and then, when it gets hot, it's like magic. It can turn into anything you want — a horseshoe, a door knocker, a gate latch.'

'But it's no life for a lovely young girl. You should be enjoying yourself, dancing, meeting people your own age — young men.'

'A husband, you mean.'

'And what's wrong with that, girl?' Ada plonked the teapot down so hard the lid rattled. 'I couldn't believe it when I heard you were working with your father. Other girls your age already have a home, babies . . . '

'Even if that's what I wanted, there's not much chance these days with all the young men off to the war.'

'Not much chance while you're working in the forge either. Who's going to look at girl with smuts on her face and hands like a navvy?'

Tilly would never admit it, but the thought had crossed her mind, especially since Nathan Miller had come to work at the forge. He had only just finished his apprenticeship with the blacksmith in the neighbouring village of Wendon when his employer had died suddenly.

Nathan, who had become an expert farrier, had gone to work on a farm looking after the horses. He had stayed for a few months until he heard that Ben Masters needed an assistant.

Tilly had been furious when Pa had taken him on. Why did he need an assistant when he had her?

Ben reassured her. 'I couldn't manage without you, lass. But I can't cope with the big draught horses these days and you're not experienced enough yet. Young Nathan has a way with them. Besides, there's work enough for three of us.'

Her father was right. The three of them did work well together and, Tilly had to admit, her life had seemed brighter since Nathan had come on the scene. She told herself she only admired him for his skill in the forge.

But why did she get this strange feeling whenever he was around — a fluttering in her stomach, shortness of breath, her cheeks flushing when he spoke to her? The problem was, she didn't know if Nathan felt the same about her — he always treated her just like a work mate.

She tried to concentrate on what her aunt was saying, at the same time wondering where Nathan had got to. He had gone into town earlier to deliver and install a gate but he should have been back long since.

She jumped when she heard her aunt mention his name. 'And what about that young Nathan Miller? I heard your father had taken him on. So where is he? Skiving off somewhere, I suppose. Can't trust these young lads to do a proper day's work these days.'

'He'll be back soon. He really does work hard, aunt.'

'Well, that's good because your father's going to need a good assistant when you're no longer here to help him.'

'What do you mean, aunt?'

'Haven't you listened to a word I've said? I want you to come and live with me. I get lonely since my husband died. And the girl I had has gone into the factory — making bullets, can you believe.' Ada rolled her eyes. 'I don't know what the world's coming to. She was perfectly comfortable with me and, as I told her, she was doing her bit for the war effort by helping me with my fund-raising activities.'

'But, aunt, I can't leave the forge. Pa can't manage without me.'

'Of course he can. He's got that Nathan now and surely one of the village women could clean and cook for him?'

Tilly wasn't quite sure what her aunt wanted from her. 'Do you mean me to come and work for you — to replace the other girl?' she asked.

'Of course not. I have Dora, my maid, and Cook, as well as a daily woman — though who knows when they'll take it into their heads to go into the factories.' She sighed. 'No — I want a companion. Besides, you're my only relative. Why shouldn't I give a home to my dear sister's only child?'

'But I have a home, aunt.' Tilly tried not to sound ungrateful but she couldn't help wondering why her aunt hadn't visited before if she had really been so fond of her sister. Was it just because her former companion had left her in the lurch?

Ada's eyes swept round the simple

cottage room. 'But I can give you so much more than — this.' She waved a hand, taking in the scrubbed kitchen table, the cooking range, the hand pump over the sink. 'You'd have your own bathroom, hot water, no cooking or cleaning. Surely it would be a better life for you.'

'I'm sorry, aunt. I've tried to explain how I love my work in the forge. I hope to be as good a blacksmith as Pa one day. I know it's not the usual job for a woman but I love it.'

Ada drained her tea and pushed the cup away. 'You're right, girl. I don't understand.' She stood up abruptly. 'Well, I won't give up. Maybe you'll come to your senses and take up my offer some day.'

But Tilly knew she wouldn't change her mind. It had always been her dream to work alongside Pa and to take over from him one day, just as he had taken over from his father. It didn't matter that she was a girl. She was strong and willing and, as Pa said, she had the 'eye'

— could see the finished article in the piece of iron before it even started to glow and soften, ready to be forged into shape.

Her mother, who had flouted convention herself to marry the village blacksmith instead of the prosperous landowner her parents had picked out for her, had always said that if Tilly was happy, so was she. And when she died a few years ago, there had been no question about it.

From that day Tilly had worked alongside her father, fitting in her housekeeping duties whenever there was a slack period in the forge. Her father agreed that a little bit of dust on the mantelpiece or sheets changed once a fortnight instead of every week, didn't really matter.

The villagers, shocked at first, gradually grew accustomed to seeing the girl in her leather apron, her hair tied back, face smudged with soot, wielding the heavy sledge hammer. Besides, with so many men now conscripted into the army, more and more women were doing work that had once been deemed unfit for them.

Ada was still going on about it and it was a relief when Ben came into the cottage. When Tilly had poured his tea and he was seated at the kitchen table, he once more demanded to know why she was there. 'It's the first time you've showed any interest in Tilly since her mother died. Why now?' he asked when Ada had explained.

'I heard you'd taken on an assistant recently so I thought maybe you could spare her.'

'But does Tilly want to live in town?' he asked with a twinkle in his eye as if he already knew the answer. 'What do you say, lass?'

'I've already told Aunt Ada that I don't want to leave you, Pa. Please don't make me go.'

Ben shrugged. 'You see, Ada. Tilly is happy here.'

'Nevertheless, Ben, you know how I feel about your daughter doing this work. It's just not seemly.'

Tilly's job was to keep the house clean and cook her father's meals, not to act as apprentice to her father — at least that's what Ada thought. Tilly just hoped that her father wasn't coming round to her way of thinking, especially now that he had an assistant in the forge.

Ben sighed, the twinkle gone. 'I know you don't approve, Ada,' he said, 'but at the moment I do need the extra pair of hands. I don't like letting people down and with all this extra work from the army, it's hard fitting in the jobs for my regular customers.'

'I thought that's why you took young Nathan on, useless big lummock that he is.'

'He's a good lad and it's lucky I heard that the blacksmith over Wendon way had died and Nathan had to give up smithing. He was wasted on that farm.' Ben drained his tea and stood up. 'Better get on. That army captain will probably be here again in the morning, with more horses to be shod before they ship them off to France.' He turned at the door. 'No rush, lass. Stay and entertain your aunt.'

Tilly winced at the mention of France. More young men were being conscripted every day and she knew it was quite likely that Nathan would probably have to go soon, too. She didn't really want to think about it.

She shook her head and roused herself to ask politely if Ada wanted more tea. Relieved when she declined, Tilly stood up and followed her aunt outside. She helped the older woman into her trap and untied the pony's halter, wishing she could feel more affection for her mother's sister.

'I'll come and see you again soon, Tilly. Maybe I'll get you to change your mind. You really would have a better life in town.'

Tilly summoned a smile. 'I'll think about it, Aunt,' she said, immediately feeling guilty as Ada's face lit up and she smiled for the first time.

As the pony and trap disappeared down the lane, Tilly stood looking after her. Maybe Ada really was lonely — or did she only want a companion to replace the girl who had left? It didn't matter. She couldn't leave while Nathan was still here — and if he was conscripted into the army, there was no way she'd leave Pa to cope alone.

★ ★ ★

When Ada had gone, Tilly set about preparing a meal for her father. She cut up a neck of mutton, sliced onions and chopped the carrots for a stew. As she pumped water to add to the pot, she couldn't help thinking that manhandling the pump handle was no different from working the bellows in the forge. What made one of them 'women's work' and the other 'man's work'? And who made the rules, anyway?

She made some dumplings and dropped them into the pot of stew which had started to simmer on the back of the range, glancing through the open cottage door and wondering if Nathan was back from his errand. She added a few herbs from the bunch which hung from a beam and sniffed the fragrant aroma that arose as she lifted the lid.

She was glad she'd made extra. It was too far for Nathan to go home for his meal and come back again. Sometimes he brought his own food, but a hunk of bread and cheese wasn't enough to sustain a man working at the forge. *Any excuse to spend more time in his company,* she chided herself, with a wry smile.

When she heard his voice in the yard she felt once more that peculiar fluttering in the pit of her stomach and she had to force herself not to rush outside. Taking a few deep breaths, she finished what she was doing before smoothing her hair and strolling towards the forge.

The young man glanced round as she approached. 'Don't know why I bothered to come back,' he said. 'Your pa says you helped him finish off Farmer Johnson's harrow.' His broad grin belied his words and Tilly responded in kind.

'Someone's got to do the work round here while you go gallivanting off into town,' she retorted, trying to cover her mirth with a serious frown.

Ben put down his hammer and wiped his brow. 'If you two are done gossiping, I need a hand here. Tilly, get some more coal in, lass. And you, Nathan, this bar's about ready for striking.' As usual he'd no sooner finished one job than it was on with the next.

Tilly went to the small shed at the side of the forge and filled the wheelbarrow with coal. The store was getting low and she wondered when they'd be able to get any more. The fuel shortage was getting worse, and the winter ahead promised to be a long and hard one. Last year's rationing had sent them foraging in the nearby woods to keep the cottage warm, saving the coal for the smithy. They had to keep the forge fired up all the time if they wanted to earn a living.

She tipped the barrow-load of coal into the bin, then took a shovelful and spread it around the edge of the forge-bed. Nathan took the tongs and pushed it towards the centre, spreading out the already glowing coals to ensure an even heat. She watched the fire change colour from cherry red to white hot, knowing the exact moment that her father would thrust the iron bar into flames. It still seemed like magic to her, the way he could tell the exact degree of heat needed for each different task. But she was learning more each day. It wouldn't be long before she'd be able to judge it as well as Pa or Nathan could.

She was sure she was ready to try doing more intricate work. She had already learned to forge the different types of horseshoe under Pa's guidance. When would he let her try one of the bigger jobs — perhaps a fancy wrought iron gate like the one at the entrance to the vicarage which had been made by her grandfather?

Everywhere you looked in Lydford and for miles around there was evidence of Grandad's and Pa's skill with iron. Tilly felt so proud whenever she crossed the green and saw the shiny new handle Pa had made for the village pump — not that it was really necessary now that most people had water laid on in their houses. But it was still used to fill the horse trough which stood on the other side of the road outside the Eight Bells, its wrought iron inn sign another example of her grandfather's work. One day, she told herself, she'd be making things like that — not just pumping the bellows, shovelling coal and making horseshoes.

The three of them worked together in silence for a while, each knowing exactly what had to be done. When the next job was finished, Ben put down his hammer and stretched, rubbing his back.

'So, your aunt's gone, has she? Wonder when she'll be back.'

'I told her it was no use — she'll never persuade me to leave the forge, Pa,' Tilly said determinedly.

'I'd let you go if you really wanted to — you know that, Tilly.'

She risked a glance at Nathan. Would he be sorry if she went to live in town? It didn't matter. She simply couldn't imagine any other life than this.

'Pa, you know I love working with you.' She grinned, showing white teeth in a tanned face. 'We make a good team, don't we?'

'Aye, lass. But in some ways I agree with your aunt.'

Tilly's smile faded. Ever since she was a child she'd loved helping her father — breaking up the coals with a hammer and feeding them into the fire, working the bellows and holding the iron bars steady while her father struck them with the heavy mallet.

It had been her proudest moment when he had allowed her to shape her very first horseshoe, a heavy clumsy-looking thing meant for a cart horse. Now she was adept at making the lighter, more elegantly wrought riding shoes. Ben had encouraged her, lovingly teaching her the tricks of his trade. She'd always thought he couldn't do without her. She remembered when her mother had died and Aunt Ada had turned up at the forge, determined to take Tilly to live with her. But even the first time, the girl had dug her heels in. 'Pa needs me,' she'd said.

And Ben had agreed, refusing to part with his beloved daughter. Now, he seemed to be having second thoughts.

★ ★ ★

Nathan had hardly dared look up when Tilly came back into the smithy with the coal. He concentrated on keeping up the regular beat as he and Ben took turns striking the hot iron.

Harvest time was over and the farmers around Lydford were anxious to get their ploughshares and other tools mended ready for ploughing and sowing the winter wheat. Each coulter blade must be sharpened, new metal welded on where necessary, then hammered and polished with sandstone until the join was well nigh invisible.

It was important work and they must be finished by the time the farmers came to collect them early the next morning. Nathan and Ben had been known to work right through the night at busy times like these.

But it wasn't tiredness that made Nathan's hammer falter. He was wondering how he would break the news to Ben Masters — and to Tilly. Now, he was regretting his impulsive action, especially when he heard that Tilly's aunt had been here, promising her a better life than slaving away at the forge. Suppose she gave in and went to live in the big house in town while he was away? She was sure to meet some man who could offer her so much more than he could.

Well, it was too late now. He had been walking across the town square when a clatter of hooves had him leaping out of the way. A captain in the Sussex Regiment, seated on a fine bay mare, was issuing orders to his men. They had rounded up what looked to Nathan like every horse in the county.

He grabbed the arm of a passing soldier. 'Where are they taking them?'

'To France, of course,' the soldier answered.

Nathan made to move on but as he turned away he noticed one of the horses limping. 'That mare needs seeing to,' he said.

'What do you mean?'

'Looks like she's got a stone in her hoof.'

'What do you know about it?' the man sneered.

'I'm a farrier — I shoe horses,' Nathan replied, annoyed at the soldier's tone. He turned away, irritated, but a shout from across the square stopped him walking off.

'Oi, you! A farrier, you say? Just the sort of young man we need.' A burly sergeant came over and looked Nathan up and down. 'In fact a fine young lad like you should already be in the army.'

'I'll go when I'm called,' Nathan said.

'Well, I'm calling you now. Take a look at that mare. We want them all fit before we take them down to the port.'

Reluctantly, Nathan had lifted the mare's hoof and removed the offending pebble with the gouge he always carried with him. As he worked, the captain trotted up and asked what was going on. When the sergeant explained, the officer said, 'You might as well take a look at the rest of them while you're here.'

'I'm not a vet,' Nathan protested. 'I only know about shoeing.'

'Well, you seem to know horses. How about signing on with us?' said the captain eagerly.

Almost without thinking, Nathan had nodded. He didn't want to leave Tilly. But it was getting harder every day to be so near her, knowing it was only a matter of time before he was called up. How could he ask her to marry him when he wasn't sure if he even had a future?

So many of his friends had gone off to the trenches, never to return. Everyone had said it wouldn't be a long war but more than three years later things were worse than ever. He couldn't imagine what it was like out there. But at least by volunteering now, he'd be working with the animals he loved and doing work he was good at.

The ploughshare was welded to Ben's satisfaction and Nathan turned to plunge it into the tank of cold water that stood to one side of the fire.

'Better get started on polishing that one, lad, while I sort out the next job,' Ben instructed.

Tilly shovelled some more coal onto the forge bed and put the shovel down. 'I'd better go and take a look at that stew. Don't want it sticking to the bottom of the pot.'

'Right, lass. We'll be in soon.'

When she'd gone, Nathan took a deep breath. 'I'll finish this but then I'll have to get off home.'

Before he could continue, Ben straightened and glared at him. 'Home? When there's work to be done? What's got into you, lad?'

'I'm sorry, master. I don't know how to tell you. I've signed on — I'm off to France tomorrow. And I must go home and break the news to my mother.'

Ben sighed. 'So you got your calling-up papers then? Why didn't you speak up before? You must have known you'd be off soon.'

'I wasn't called up — I volunteered,' Nathan blurted.

'What'd you want to go and do that for?'

'It was the horses. They were herding them into the square at Lydmouth ready to take them down to the harbour. The sergeant called me over. I knew I'd be called up sooner or later and I thought if I volunteered then and there, like, I'd be able to work with the horses.'

'Well, as you say, it had to happen some time.' Ben sighed. 'How am I going to manage with only a slip of a girl to help me and all this extra work?'

'Tilly's as good as any man. She works as hard as you and me.'

'You're right, I couldn't manage without her. But I wish you'd given me time to think about taking on an apprentice.' He turned away muttering, 'Springing it on me like that.'

Nathan mumbled an apology, already sorry he'd acted so impulsively. How could he bear to leave Tilly?

No use telling himself she wasn't for him. Even if her father agreed to the match, her aunt was sure to stick her nose in. Besides, he'd have been called up anyway. Still, he could have waited. Every moment spent with her was precious. If only he had the courage to tell her so.

He grabbed the sandstone and began polishing furiously. Soon the ploughshare was smooth and shiny, no sign of the join. It would cut through the stoniest soil like butter. *As good as new,* he thought with satisfaction, momentarily distracted from his troubles.

Ben lifted a piece of metal from the fire, doused it in water and laid down his tongs. He inspected the ploughshare Nathan had been working on. 'That'll do, lad,' he said. 'Better get off back to Wendon. Your mother's not going to be pleased with your news, so break it gently.'

'Thanks, master. Say goodbye to Tilly for me.' Nathan couldn't bear to face her. He grabbed his jacket off the hook behind the door and hurried across the village green, hoping she wouldn't look out of the cottage door as he quickly passed by.

★ ★ ★

Dusk was falling and the stew was ready, the dumplings light and fluffy. Tilly lit the lamp that hung over the scrubbed table and looked out of the cottage door towards the forge. Where were they? She set the table and decided to call the men in to supper. If she didn't they'd likely work all night without a break. Smithing was heavy work and they needed their food.

As she stepped outside, she saw Ben came out of the forge, but there was no sign of Nathan. 'Isn't Nathan having supper with us?' she called.

'He's gone home,' Ben replied.

Home? With so much work waiting? What had got into him? Tilly's heart sank. Perhaps he didn't want to spend time with her. Before she could ask why he had left early Ben said, 'He asked me to say goodbye to you.'

'Well, he'll be back later if there's so much work to do. Why didn't he stay for supper?'

Ben busied himself washing his hands at the pump over the sink. He cleared his throat. 'The lad's gone and joined up — he's off to France first thing in the morning.'

Tilly gasped, almost dropping the

heavy stew pot. She plonked it down on the table, her hands shaking. 'France? Why didn't he say something before? He can't just go off without saying goodbye.' She couldn't help it. The tears welled up and she sat down heavily.

Her father sat down opposite and took her hands in his own. 'Don't take on so, lass. You knew it had to happen sooner or later. I know you'll miss him — I will too. Now I'll have to find another lad to train up.'

'I'm not thinking about the forge, Pa.' Tilly bit her lip. 'You don't understand,' she muttered.

Her father nodded. 'I understand more than you think,' he said. 'I've seen which way the wind's blowing. But you're still too young to be thinking that way, my girl.'

Tilly wanted to deny it. What did an old man like her father know about hearts beating faster at the sight of someone, about dreaming of kisses? She sniffed and wiped her nose.

Ben patted her hand. 'Come on, Tilly love. Dish up that stew. It smells delicious. Can't wait to tuck in.'

She ladled the meat and its rich thick gravy into the bowls, sawed off a few hunks of bread and picked up her spoon. But she couldn't eat.

She thought of the long lists read out in church each Sunday, remembered those few who had returned to the village, wounded, missing arms, legs. That couldn't happen to Nathan.

Oh, why had he volunteered? The war could have been over before he was forced to go.

Her father echoed her thoughts. 'He should have waited for his call-up,' he said. 'At least I'd have had time to get someone else. But he said he had to go when he saw the horses.'

'Horses? What do they have to do with anything?'

'They were rounding them up in the market square. They need someone to look after them. He knows horses, loves them you might say.'

Loves them more than me, Tilly thought. 'If he's so fond of horses, he should have stayed on the farm where he was working after his old master died,' she said sulkily.

'He almost did, until I met him at market and told him he shouldn't be wasting the valuable horse skills he'd already learned there,' said Ben.

'If he worked on the farm, he wouldn't have to go to war at all,' Tilly said with a catch in her throat. But then she would never have got to know him, fallen in love with him, she thought. At least they'd had that time together, working and laughing, enjoying each other's company. No one could take that away. And he would come back — he would, he must.

2

Tilly had spent a sleepless night. Why hadn't Nathan said goodbye to her? Despite their easy friendship, the laughter and camaraderie as they worked together, perhaps she had imagined that he was beginning to care for her in the same way that she did for him?

Early the next morning as she was stirring the breakfast porridge, rubbing eyes which were gritty from lack of sleep, she heard the clatter of hooves in the yard. Probably a farmer come to collect one of his tools, she thought, but she couldn't stop the little flare of hope that Nathan had come to say goodbye. She dropped the spoon and rushed outside.

But the tall, handsome man who had just dismounted from the huge black stallion was a stranger.

Swallowing her disappointment, she asked, 'Can I help you?'

'He's lost a shoe — where's the smith?'

'My father's busy at the moment. I can take a look at him,' Tilly said.

The man looked her up and down and his lip curled in a sneer. 'You? What do you know about shoeing?'

Tilly clenched her fists at her sides and tightened her lips. 'I probably know more than you think.'

'And why's a pretty girl like you doing a man's work?'

'Probably because all the men are away fighting the war,' Tilly replied sharply, noting the fine cut of his hacking jacket, the snowy cravat at his throat, and wondering why he wasn't in uniform. She was about to ask just that when he suddenly smiled, revealing even white teeth and a sparkle in his dark eyes.

He laughed. 'A girl with spirit — I like that. Well, girl, I'm very particular about who deals with my horses but

I'm a long way from home and Thunder here needs a new shoe, so . . . '

As they talked Tilly had noticed the horse fidgeting and realised it was the left foreleg that needed attention. She approached the animal and took its bridle, stroking the soft nose and murmuring to calm it. 'My father will fit the new shoe,' she said, 'but I can do the preparation.' She lifted the horse's hoof and examined the underside, noting that it needed a thorough cleaning where grass and small stones had become embedded. 'You must have ridden him quite a way in this condition,' she said, straightening up.

She handed the bridle back to him and went inside the smithy to fetch her tools. Ben looked up. 'Who were you talking to?'

'Man with a horse to shoe, a beautiful hunter, too,' she said.

'Right girl, make a start and I'll be out in a minute.' He paused. 'Who is it, anyone we know?'

'Stranger to me, Pa.'

'I thought all the horses had been requisitioned by the army,' said Ben.

Tilly had been thinking the same thing as she set out her tools and started work. Who was this man and how had he managed to hang on to this lovely stallion when horses had all but disappeared from the surrounding countryside?

She wanted to ask but when she looked up at him, he was staring at her with a slight smile on his handsome face. She hastily looked away and carried on with her work. She picked the hoof clean and trimmed it with the paring knife before smoothing the rough edges with a rasp. She kept her head bent until her father came out of the smithy.

'Lovely animal,' Ben said, patting Thunder's neck. 'You're not from round these parts then?'

'Not too far away. I'm from the other side of Lydmouth — had business over here — not that it's any concern of yours, my man.'

Tilly breathed in sharply, annoyed at his tone. She gave a final sweep of the rasp and straightened up. 'All ready, Pa.'

Ben nodded and went back into the smithy where several ready-made shoes hung on the wall. He selected one and measured it against the stallion's hoof. Now it just needed finishing off. Nodding at Tilly to start the bellows, he heated the iron shoe and moulded it to fit.

While they worked, the stranger leaned against the door post, the horse's bridle in his hand, watching them intently.

Usually, Tilly didn't mind. Most of their customers were known to her and she had become used to their curiosity about the girl blacksmith. But she found this man's quizzical stare most disconcerting. It was a relief when Ben tapped the final nail into place and straightened up.

'That should see you all right now, sir,' he said.

The man examined the new shoe. 'An excellent job,' he said, leaping up onto the horse's back. He fumbled in his pocket and leaned down, handing a small card to Ben. 'Send your bill there. I'll see it's paid straight away.'

Before Ben could answer he had leapt astride the horse, wheeled round and galloped away across the green.

'That's the last we'll see of him — or his money,' Ben said, wiping his face and neck with the old cloth which always hung out of his back pocket.

'The cheek of the man,' Tilly said, gathering up her tools and putting them in their proper place inside the forge. 'And why isn't he in the army like all the other young men?'

'It's nothing to do with us. Now, what about a bite to eat, lass? I'm famished.' He followed her into the cottage and tucked into his porridge while Tilly cut bread and fried some bacon. Sitting down opposite him, she picked up the card which the stranger had left. 'Richard Lacey, Lydsey

Manor, Lydmouth,' she read aloud.

'Aye, I know who he is now — Sir Thomas's younger son. The older one is an officer in the Sussex regiment and I believe young Richard stayed behind to manage the estate. His father's too old and infirm to do it himself. The family's got influence, though — that's how he managed to hang on to that fine hunter of his.'

They finished their meal and Tilly cleared away while Ben went back to the forge. She poured the last of the hot water into the enamel bowl and refilled the kettle, pushing it to the back of the range. As she began to wash the dishes a shadow fell across the open doorway.

'Am I too late for breakfast, Tilly?'

Thoughts of the handsome stranger fled and she whirled round. 'Nathan! You're here. Did you change your mind?' Before he could answer she took in the uniform he was now wearing, the stiff khaki battledress and shiny new boots. Her face fell. 'You're really off, then?'

He nodded. 'I shouldn't really be here but I just couldn't go without saying goodbye.'

'I don't know why you have to go at all,' she said, tears welling up as she struggled to keep her feelings from showing.

'I'm only doing my duty, as lots of others are. At least this way I'm with the horses. If I'd waited they could have put me in those awful tanks they're using now. I couldn't bear that, being shut in.'

'I understand,' she said. But she didn't really. Why did men have to fight wars anyway?

'What about this breakfast you mentioned? I've only got half an hour.'

'There's some bacon left. I'll put it in a sandwich for you.'

He only took a few mouthfuls before draining the mug of tea she had set before him and pushing his chair back. 'I'm sorry, Tilly, I must go. Better speak to your father too before I leave.'

She wanted to hold him back, willing

him to say that he loved her, that he would miss her.

She followed him outside, watching as he checked the saddle and bridle of the horse he had arrived on. She stroked the animal's nose. 'He's lovely. Where did you get him?'

'He's one of the horses we requisitioned yesterday. I said he needed shoeing,' he said.

So, he had come to use the forge, not to see her, Tilly thought.

'Better get on with it then,' she said, turning away.

He laughed. 'It was just an excuse, Tilly. I wanted to come and say goodbye. But I can't stay — I said it wouldn't take long. We'll be off soon.'

Tilly's heart lurched. So he had come to see her after all. Why did he have to go? She might never see him again. She thought again of the boys she had known since childhood who had gone off so cheerfully and were never coming back. A lump rose in her throat and she fought to hold back the tears that threatened.

Nathan took her hand. 'Please don't cry. I'm going to be all right. When we get over there they'll have a forge and all the equipment we need behind the lines.' His irrepressible grin flashed out once more. 'So you see, Tilly my love, you don't need to worry about me.'

My love — had he said my love? She blushed but managed to sound careless. 'Who says I'll worry about you?'

He squeezed her hand more tightly. 'Tilly, I don't want you to worry, but I want you to think about me. And when I get home . . . '

'Nathan, lad, come to say goodbye?' Ben's hearty voice interrupted and Nathan dropped her hand quickly. Tilly sighed. He'd leave now without saying what she longed to hear.

Ben slapped the younger man on the shoulder. 'Good luck, lad. Come back safe.' He turned to Tilly. 'Don't hang about, lass. Work's awaiting.'

He disappeared into the smithy and Nathan rolled his eyes. 'Good timing,'

42

he said, taking her hand again. 'Tilly, I wanted to do this right, but there's no time. I just want to tell you . . . ' He hesitated, then took a deep breath. 'I'll miss you. Will you let me write to you?'

Tilly let her breath out. He hadn't said it. But perhaps this was as much as she could expect for now. At least he'd miss her — and he would write. 'Of course, Nathan, I'll miss you too,' she said.

He pulled her towards him, planted a swift kiss on her lips and, before she had time to react, leapt up on the horse and galloped away. At the end of the lane, he turned in the saddle and waved once. Then he was gone.

Tilly stood for a long time staring after him, fingers to her mouth, still feeling the imprint of his lips on hers.

It wasn't how she had imagined a declaration of love would be. But she was sure that was what he had meant. In the short time they had worked together she had come know him well and realised that he was quite shy, hiding this beneath a veneer of cheeky banter.

* * *

With Nathan gone Tilly had to do even more work in the forge. At one time she would have been pleased. It had always been her ambition to take over from her father one day. But although she loved the work, she hadn't realised quite how exhausted she would be at the end of each day — what with the cooking and the washing, not to mention coping with the food shortages. Even if she'd had time to go into town there was little in the shops and there was talk of more rationing. Luckily some of their customers still paid in kind so they had plenty of butter and eggs, and even the odd rabbit or fowl.

Most of the horses on the neighbouring farms had been requisitioned by the army and shipped off to France so there was little shoeing to be done, but there was still plenty of work. The farmers were now using traction engines more than ever and some had even invested in the new-fangled tractors. Things were always going wrong. The stony soil in these parts meant that the ploughshares, harrows and drills often became worn and cracked. Ben and Tilly's skills were much in demand.

Keeping busy meant that there was little time to brood, although Tilly still found herself looking up in anticipation whenever the post boy wobbled down the lane on his bicycle. But the weeks went by and there was no letter.

There was another visit from Aunt Ada however and her first words were guaranteed to fire up Tilly's temper. 'Goodness me, girl, you look worn out.'

Of course she was worn out, like everyone else in the village. With all the young men gone, everyone was struggling to keep going. Miss Lillywhite, the postmistress, had lost her assistant to the factory in town and the post was now delivered by a cheeky young lad who should have still been at school.

Girls were working on the farms now, doing the work of men too.

The manpower shortage had affected Tilly and her father as well. Not long after Nathan had left, the village wheelwright had died suddenly. With no son to take over, his work was now being shared between Sid, the local carpenter, and the smithy.

Ben had been unable to find a new apprentice either, so they were working harder than ever. Not that Tilly minded. She scarcely had time to think about Nathan until she went to bed. And even then, when she tried to re-live those last precious moments with him, she soon fell into an exhausted sleep.

Before she could answer her aunt however, Ben said, 'No time to stop and chat, Ada. If you want a cup of tea, you'd better go indoors and put the kettle on. Tilly will be in as soon as we've finished this.' He nodded to Tilly to hold the iron steady and gave it a hefty blow.

She couldn't help grinning as her

father continued to hit the iron bar with more force than was really necessary. He was just as annoyed at the interruption as she was.

She straightened her face and turned to her aunt who still stood in the doorway, hands on hips, her lips pressed tightly together. 'I'll be with you in a minute, Aunt,' she said.

Inside the cottage, Ada had made the tea and was busy folding the clean tea cloths and pillow cases that hung over the rail in front of the kitchen range. 'The way your father makes you work, it's a wonder you have time to do anything in the house. There's all this ironing to do — no wonder you always look so tired.'

Tilly didn't tell her that she didn't bother to iron everything. Ada thought it was shocking enough, her doing 'man's work'. *Besides,* she thought rebelliously, *if her aunt was so concerned why didn't she offer to help? Not that she ever picked up an iron herself.* She had been left comfortably off and had servants to do everything for her.

Ada was still trying to persuade her to leave the forge. 'If you came to live with me, you'd have a room of your own. You could help with my ladies' group and meet some really nice people. I'm sure your poor mother would be turning in her grave if she could see how your father makes you work.'

Tilly couldn't stand it any longer. 'I wish I could make you understand, Aunt. Pa doesn't make me work. I do it because I enjoy it. Besides, since Nathan joined the army, there's no one else. Pa's tried to get an apprentice but all the young lads are joining up as soon as they're old enough. He can't manage on his own.'

'Well, I don't know why that lad had to volunteer. He might not have been called up for months — and this war surely can't go on much longer.' She sighed. 'Look, Tilly, I'm only thinking what's best for you. I'm sure this isn't what your mother wanted for you.'

It was no good. Her aunt would never understand. Tilly sighed and poured the tea. She stood up and filled a big mug to take out to her father. He wouldn't come into the house for a break until Ada had gone.

'She been on at you again?' he asked, taking a grateful sip of tea.

Tilly nodded and her father patted her shoulder. 'You know, lass, if you wanted to go, I wouldn't stop you. I'd get by.'

'You know how I feel about it. I'd be stifled, leading the kind of life she wants me to.'

'I understand.' He handed her the mug. 'Better get back indoors. And, Tilly, be nice to her. She only wants what she thinks is best for you.'

'That's what she said.'

Tilly went back into the cottage to find her aunt biting into a freshly-baked scone and nodding approval. 'Your mother taught you well.' She took another and spread it liberally with butter. 'Well, I must say, you live well, in spite of the food shortages.'

Tilly didn't reply, concentrating on topping up the teapot with hot water from the kettle on the range. Her aunt had sounded disapproving but she must know that often they were not paid for their work in cash but in gifts of meat and garden produce, eggs and butter.

At last Ada finished her tea and stood up, brushing the crumbs off her lap and straightening her old-fashioned bonnet. 'Well, it seems I can't talk any sense into you or that stubborn father of yours,' she said. 'But I won't give up. It's not right, a lovely girl like you spending all her days covered in dirt and ruining her hands with such rough work.'

'Lots of women are doing so-called men's work now, Aunt. With all the men being called up, someone's got to keep things going here at home.'

'I know that, Tilly. I do war work myself, as you know. My ladies' group have sent out more parcels to the Front than anyone else in the parish. Those poor boys need plenty of socks and scarves, especially with winter coming on.' She sighed. 'I must be off — I only came to see how you were getting on. I do worry about you, you know.'

'I know, Aunt.' Tilly kissed the older woman's cheek. 'I do appreciate your concern, truly.'

'Well, just so you know.' She turned and said, 'Oh, before I forget. The ladies' committee is arranging a charity ball at Lydsey Manor to raise money for the war effort. All the best people will be there. I want you to come.'

'But I can't dance and, besides, I have nothing to wear.'

'Don't worry about that. I'll get my dressmaker to run you up a ball gown. Besides, I need you there beforehand to help with the arrangements and to sell tickets. There's a lot to do, Tilly. Now, promise me you'll come.'

'I don't know, Aunt. We're so busy in the forge and Pa needs me here.'

'Surely he can spare you for just a few days.'

'I'll see what he says,' Tilly promised, hoping deep in her heart that he would say no. How could she go gallivanting off to town and leave him to do all the work? Besides, she knew it was just a ploy to get her to stay in town. But she wouldn't be bought by the promise of a ball gown and an evening of mixing with all the 'best people'.

She followed Ada outside and looked round. 'Where's your pony and trap? How did you get here?'

'Blessed army's taken my pony. Nothing I could do about it. I came on the carrier's cart. He'll pick me up at the end of the lane, so I'd better hurry.'

When she'd gone, Tilly heaved a sigh of relief. She was much too busy to sit making small talk while there was work to be done. Besides, she had hoped that there would be time to continue her letter to Nathan.

Although he hadn't written to her yet and she had no idea where to send a letter, she had got in the habit of writing a little whenever she had time, telling him about the goings on in the village, the work in the forge and the battles with her aunt. She was careful not to reveal her deepest feelings, however. She'd wait until she heard from him, try to gauge his feelings — that's if he ever wrote at all.

3

It was a fine breezy day after weeks of rain and Tilly was pegging sheets on the line that stretched between two apple trees behind the cottage, when she heard the distinctive sound of the post boy's tuneless whistle. She dropped the last of the wet linen back into the basket and ran round the side of the house, almost snatching the envelope from his hand. It was weeks since Nathan had left. Christmas was almost here and she still hadn't heard from him. But it wasn't the letter she had been longing for.

'Hey, what's the rush? It's only from your old auntie,' the boy said, grinning through the gap in his teeth. Disappointed, Tilly slowly opened the envelope, quickly scanning the contents. Nothing exciting — just a note reminding her of the New Year charity ball and her promise to attend.

But I didn't promise, Tilly thought rebelliously. She read the letter again. Maybe she would go after all. Nathan obviously didn't care, or he would have written. Besides, she deserved some fun after working so hard for weeks and she couldn't deny she was curious about Lydsey Manor. Maybe she'd meet the handsome Richard Lacey again.

She looked up to see the post boy still grinning at her. 'Well, what are you hanging around for?' she snapped.

He pulled another item from his bag. 'I suppose you want this one as well,' he said, waving it in the air.

As she went to grab it, he turned away, reading aloud from the card. 'To my sweetheart . . . '

Thoughts of Richard Lacey fled as she snatched the card from his hand. 'You're not supposed to read other people's letters. What would Miss Lillywhite say if I told her? You'd lose your job, for sure.'

The postmistress was a formidable

spinster who had little time for the lads in her employ but she had to put up with them now that the regular postmen were serving at the front. Besides which, with every family having someone in the forces, more letters were being sent than at any time in the postal service's history.

'You won't say anything, will you?' the lad pleaded.

'If you promise not to look at anything else I get,' she said darkly. She could imagine him going round the village telling all his friends about the soppy card the blacksmith's daughter had received. However, the threat to his job was enough to make him promise.

When he'd gone, Tilly tucked the card into her apron pocket and finished hanging the washing, savouring the moment when she could go indoors and read it. Despite her elation at hearing from Nathan at last, she felt embarrassed at the thought of everyone being able to see what he'd written. Why had he sent a card? Why hadn't he put it in an envelope? Well, at least he had kept his promise to write, even if it had taken him weeks to do so.

She picked up the empty laundry basket and returned to the cottage, singing under her breath. She sat down at the kitchen table and pulled the card from her pocket, fingering the fancy edging which was cut out to look like lace. In the centre was a picture of a church surrounded by a frame of roses with some words in French at the bottom. She guessed that was the name of the place. Intertwined with the roses were the words 'to my own sweetheart'. Smiling, she turned it over and read the pencil scrawl. 'Just to let you know I'm all right, working behind the lines. Thinking of you every day. Will write more later. Please send writing paper. All my love . . . '

Under his name was a row of crosses. Tilly kissed the spot where he'd written his name and tucked the card down the front of her blouse where it nestled against her heart. She sat gazing out of the window and dreaming of the day Nathan would come home. After a moment she sighed and stood up, took off her cotton apron and donned the leather one, then went to help her father in the forge.

Ben looked up from the anvil and put his hammer down. 'Good to see you looking so cheerful for a change, lass.'

'I had a card from Nathan.'

'Oh, what's he got to say for himself then?'

Tilly blushed. 'Nothing much — just letting us know he's all right.'

'Am I going to be allowed to read it then?' he retorted playfully.

'No! — It's just a card with a picture of a church.'

Ben grinned and went over to the forge, where he started raking the coals. 'Well, lass, are we going to get any work done today then?'

As she bent to shovel the coal, Tilly could feel the rough card against her skin and a surge of happiness went through her. Nathan might be sparing with words but the card with its printed message said it all. Now she just had to pray that he would return safely.

Daydreaming about their future after the war was over, she didn't hear the horse cantering up to the smithy and she jumped as a loud voice called from outside. 'Anyone about?'

Ben was absorbed in hammering a tricky piece of ironwork so Tilly dropped her shovel and went outside. Richard Lacey was leaning against the post where he had tied his horse.

'Don't tell me Thunder needs another shoe?' said Tilly.

'No, I came to see you, Miss Masters,' he said with his insolent grin.

'Me? I can't imagine why.'

'Oh, I'm sure you can,' he drawled, looking her up and down.

As she felt herself beginning to blush, he laughed, showing his even white teeth. 'I'm teasing you, Miss Masters,' he said. 'Actually, I came to add my pleas to those of your aunt. I did not realise you were Mrs Bradford's niece.

We all admire her tireless efforts on behalf of our men over in France. And she tells me she has asked for your help with the ball which is being held at Lydsey Manor.'

'I have already told my aunt I cannot be spared from the forge. My father needs me here,' Tilly said.

'I'm sure if I were to speak to your father he would agree to let you go.'

'Please don't do that, sir. He really can't manage on his own.'

'What a pity. I would have enjoyed showing you around the estate.' He mounted his horse and rode away, leaving Tilly feeling a little bewildered. Had he meant what she thought he had? No — men like Richard Lacey had only one interest in girls from humble backgrounds. Besides, she was spoken for. Still, she couldn't help admitting to being curious about Lydsey Manor and its occupants.

As she picked up her shovel and resumed work, her father asked who she had been talking to. Without quite knowing why, she said it was someone who had lost his way. Ben didn't comment. With so many movements of troops these days, strangers were much more common than they had been before the war.

They finished the ploughshare they had been working on and Ben straightened and rubbed his back. 'Time for a break, lass. Let's have a bite to eat before Sid gets here with those wheels for Farmer Bray's cart. I've already got the iron hoops ready. They just need to be heated again and adjusted for size. Sid and I might be able to manage if he brings his lad with him. Otherwise I'll need your help.'

They had finished their bread and cheese when Sid, the village carpenter, arrived. He'd brought his young son with him so Tilly was free to finish her household chores, although sometimes it took three or four pairs of hands to fix the iron tyres onto the wooden wheels before dousing them in the village pond to shrink the metal to a tight fit.

With the cottage clean and tidy, Tilly went to the door and stood for a few moments watching the men at work. They seemed to be managing quite well without her help so she took Nathan's card out of her bodice and once more read the pitifully few words he had written. At least she could reply now she had an address.

She went to the dresser and took out the letter she had started a few days ago. After reading it through, she picked up her pencil to add a final few lines. She began to tell him about her aunt's invitation and Richard Lacey's insistence that she attend the ball. But something stopped her. Instead, she wrote, 'I hope you meant the words that were printed on the card you sent me and that I truly am your own sweetheart. I am thinking of you and praying for you every day and longing for your safe return.'

When she'd signed the letter she went to the jar on the dresser and counted the pile of coins it contained.

There was enough to buy a writing pad and some envelopes to send to Nathan. Much as she loved the pretty card he had sent, she would rather have a proper letter — one that cheeky post boys wouldn't be able to read and tease her about.

When she went outside, Ben and the carpenter had finished the cart wheels and were loading them on the wagon, while Sid's son gathered up the tools and debris left behind. Tilly left them to it and went behind the cottage to take in the washing. The stiff breeze had completely dried the sheets and she thought if she folded them carefully she would get away with not ironing them. Her father wouldn't notice, anyway.

★　★　★

Although Nathan loved working with the horses, he was beginning to wonder if he'd made the right decision in volunteering for the army. Here he was, well behind the lines and spared the horrors of the trenches, but even here, he could feel the ground shake with the bombardment, could see the acres of mud broken by the stark skeletons of tree stumps, the shells of shattered buildings.

Worst of all were the injuries to his beloved animals. By the end of 1917, many of the hundreds of horses that had shipped out with him a few months earlier had been slaughtered on the battlefield or died later from their wounds. In addition there was little food for the animals and many of them were fated to starve. So often there was nothing the veterinary surgeons could do, and the only course was to put the animal out of its misery.

Although he had recently been promoted from trooper to farrier sergeant, Nathan now found that his duties were not confined to looking after the horses' hooves. With so many animals being injured and not enough vets to go round, he was often called on to dress wounds and even assist the vets.

On this bitterly cold morning, Nathan was grooming a bay mare that had been left in his care — its rider deposited in the casualty clearing station the night before. He had cleaned and dressed the gaping hole on the horse's flank and was now brushing out the mud-encrusted tail. The air was still and his breath plumed in the cold air. For a change, no sound came from the direction of the trenches, but he knew it would not be long before the bombardment started up again. *How long could this go on?* he wondered.

The horse snickered and tossed her mane and Nathan gave an involuntary smile. If horses could think like humans, she was probably wondering the same thing.

He gave a final brush to her tail and patted her rump. 'You'll do, my beauty,' he said, turning as a veterinary officer entered the enclosure behind him and called his name.

'Miller, that one's fit to go back up the line. Take her out, then get over to the smithy. There's a whole line of mules waiting for shoes.'

'Yes, sir.' Nathan took hold of the mare's bridle and led her out and along the muddy road to where a group of horses and men waited. He rubbed her velvety nose before handing her over to a trooper, then turned away quickly. *Stupid to get so attached to an animal,* he thought, knowing that it was unlikely he'd ever see her again. And by the end of the day there would be hundreds more like her.

When he reached the smithy, his mate Ginger, a farrier from Hampshire who had joined up at the same time as Nathan, had already fired up the forge and the coals were beginning to glow.

He looked up and grinned. 'Bloody mules today, Nat. Just our luck, eh?'

Nathan grinned in return. Mules were in a class of their own and he did not relish the day's work that lay ahead. Sometimes it took two men to hold the animal still while its shoes were fitted. Luckily a couple of troopers had been detailed to assist.

Stacked in a corner of the smithy — an abandoned farm building where they had set up the forge — was a pile of ready-made shoes. Usually Nathan didn't mind cold shoeing; it was a routine task which freed his mind to wander back to happier days. But today it was bitterly cold and he was grateful for the heat from the forge when, occasionally, they would come across an animal with a slightly smaller or larger hoof and the iron would have to be heated and re-formed.

The two men worked together and the line gradually diminished. As they worked, Nathan once more began to lose himself in his work and, if it wasn't for the distant thunder of the guns, he could almost imagine that he was back in Lydford, working alongside Tilly. He smiled inwardly, remembering her determination to master the art of shaping a horse shoe and to take on the more complex work of the blacksmith. Had Ben allowed her to have her way yet? Nathan smiled. Tilly was quite adept at getting round her father.

As darkness fell, they finished with the last mule and Nathan stretched and rubbed his back. Back at the billet, after a hasty meal of stale biscuits and bully beef, he got out his stub of pencil and the last of the precious writing paper Tilly had sent him.

But as he settled down to write he hesitated. What could he tell her? There was no way he could recount some of the horrors he had seen — and he had seen some terrible things, despite being behind the lines and away from any real fighting. And by the same token, he could not make it sound as if he was having an easy time of it when so many of the lads she had known from childhood had returned home with terrible injuries — and in many cases, would not be going home at all.

In the end he told her briefly what he had been doing that day and added a few humorous comments on the nature of mules. 'No wonder they say stubborn as a mule,' he wrote. 'I can vouch for that myself. I've got the bruises to prove it.' He hoped that would make her smile.

He paused and licked his pencil. Unable to think of anything else to write, he sighed and finished with his usual phrase. 'Hoping and praying that it will not be too long before I see you again. Your loving Nathan.'

As he sealed it and wrote the address he tried to picture her, wishing he had a photograph as most of the other men did of wives and sweethearts. Her face had become blurred in his mind and he sometimes got a panicky feeling that he would not recognise her when he got home. And suppose she had changed her mind about him?

Her letters were always sweet and loving but in the last one she had told him that she was going to spend a few days with her aunt. Ada Bradford was organising a charity ball in aid of soldiers' comforts and had asked Tilly to help her. Suppose she met someone there — someone her aunt would deem a better match than a humble blacksmith?

Lost in thought, he didn't notice Ginger come into the billet until he punched him on the shoulder. 'Cheer up mate — it might never happen,' his friend said jovially.

Nathan hastily put the letter in his tunic pocket, not in the mood for Ginger's teasing. 'I'm all right — just tired is all.'

'Well, we're all tired, mate. But no use sitting here feeling sorry for ourselves. The blokes in the other billet are having a bit of a sing song. Why don't you come along and join us?'

Nathan wasn't keen on the idea but he knew Ginger would keep on at him so he stood up and grabbed his gas mask and rifle. 'Okay then — let's go.' After all, who knew when the next bombardment would start? They had to make the most of these short periods of comparative peace and quiet.

Tilly wasn't at the forge in Lydford as Nathan had imagined. Her father had allowed her a few days off to stay with her aunt and complete the arrangements for the ball. Ada was in her element ordering flowers to decorate the grand entrance hall at Lydsey Manor which was to serve as the ballroom. There were massive displays in urns on each side of the door and vases on every surface. The curving staircase also had strands of greenery entwined along the banisters and there were smaller arrangements on the tables in the dining room which led off the hall.

'Surely they have a housekeeper, Aunt?' Tilly had protested when she had been asked to help.

'Most of the servants have left to do war work and the housekeeper has been ill. Sir Thomas knows of my experience in these matters and asked me to oversee the arrangements. Since his wife died he has come to rely on me to see that things run smoothly at the manor.'

She gave a secretive little smile and Tilly, with a sudden flash of insight, realised that her aunt was hoping for more from the relationship. She had been lonely since the death of her husband and had thrown herself into charitable works. In a way, the war had given her a new lease of life.

Tilly hoped the older woman would find happiness, although she could not imagine anyone wanting to marry an old and infirm man like Sir Thomas for all his wealth and standing in the county. But status and position were everything to her aunt.

To her surprise, Tilly found she was enjoying herself. It was a nice change to curl her hair and wear pretty dresses. And, after just a few days of rubbing her aunt's scented cream into her hands, the ingrained dirt from the forge was beginning to disappear.

Then there was Lydsey Manor, the

grandest house she had ever been in. She wandered through the great hall, storing the images up in her mind — the crystal chandeliers, the huge fireplace with its carved stone overmantel, the sweeping staircase with its wrought iron balusters intricately decorated with gold leaf.

As she ran her hand over the delicate ironwork, she dreamed of one day creating something like this — a thing of beauty but with a useful purpose behind it. She couldn't wait to tell Nathan all about it.

But that evening, as she sat down to write to him in the study of her aunt's elegant townhouse in Lydmouth, she could not find the right words. How could she describe such beauties to him when she knew what he must be going through? There had been nothing else from him since the postcard and she was beginning to think he did not really care for her. When she'd commented to her father that she had expected a letter before now, he reassured her. 'We know what it's like out there from the newspapers, lass,' he said. 'Letters are bound to get lost in the post — that's if he gets the chance to write at all.'

Tilly had nodded sadly, realising that he was probably right. Besides, whatever happened, she would keep writing to him. For, from what her aunt said, it was obvious that this war wasn't the noble enterprise all those young men had envisaged when they'd marched off so gaily in 1914. Writing cheerily encouraging letters was her way of keeping his spirits up.

She chewed the end of her pencil and finally managed to write a couple of pages. She told him how much she missed him and how hard her aunt was making her work, checking things off on the long lists she had made and running errands in the town. 'I can't wait to get back to Pa and the forge,' she wrote.

As she formed the words, she knew it was true. This was just an interlude — she did not want the sort of life her aunt had. She despised the ladies on

the ball committee with their conde-
scending attitude and their conviction
that they were superior to everyone
else. The simple farm folk and villagers
of Lydford were more to her liking.

She signed her name with her usual
declaration of love and leaned back in
her chair, smiling as she pictured the
day when Nathan would be home and
they would once more work side by side
in the village smithy.

The door opened and she sat up
straight, covering the page with her
hand as her aunt came in.

'Have you finished going through
those lists?' Ada inquired.

'Yes, aunt. Everything is in order. The
rest of the flowers will be delivered to
the manor early tomorrow. Cook has
the sweetmeats made and she has managed to get two girls from the village to
come in and lay everything out.'

'I hope she has instructed them
properly,' Ada said with a frown. 'These
girls have had no training at all.'

'I'm sure Cook will explain what they

have to do. Besides, you have done your best and I'm sure everyone will understand that things are not the same as they were before the war. All the guests have the same problem themselves — they are having to learn how to do without the armies of people who once waited on them.'

'You're right, Tilly. We are all having to make sacrifices.' She sighed.

Tilly bit her lip and turned away, wishing she had the courage to say what she really thought. Nathan and hundreds like him were the ones making sacrifices. How could having to do without a ladies' maid be regarded in the same way as the lives of the lads she'd known as a child? As for eating and drinking and dancing, however much money it raised for the war effort, it could hardly compare with the simple lives of the villagers that Tilly called her friends. Why couldn't they just give money without all this?

Of course, she could not voice these thoughts to Aunt Ada. She'd never understand. She folded her letter and stood up. 'I'm very tired, Aunt. I think I'll go up now.'

'Yes, we have a busy day ahead of us.'

As Tilly passed her in the doorway, Ada took hold of her hand. 'You're a good girl, Tilly. You have been such a help these past couple of days.' She stroked the now soft hand. 'Don't forget to use the cream I gave you — see what a difference it has made already. Such a pretty girl, such a waste,' she murmured sadly.

Tilly pulled her hand away. It was true she had enjoyed this little holiday from her hard working life, but it was not the real world. She knew the novelty would soon pall but her aunt was unconvinced. Would she never stop trying to persuade her to give up her old life and abandon her father?

★　★　★

By the evening of the next day Tilly was exhausted. Nothing seemed to meet her aunt's exacting standards and she just wished for the whole thing to be over so that she could go home.

At last everything was ready and Tilly and her aunt retreated to one of the maids' attic rooms where they had been told they could change into their party dresses. After being treated as a servant for the past few days, Tilly had been surprised when Ada told her that they were on the guest list.

'Sir Thomas insisted,' Ada said, her cheeks flushing. 'Such an opportunity for you, dear. All the county people will be here. Now, don't forget what I told you — whatever you do, do not mention the forge.'

Tilly bit her lip. 'Suppose someone asks where I'm from?'

'Just say you are my niece, staying with me in Lydmouth — there's no need to elaborate.'

Tilly nodded, but she was unhappy at the thought of being deceitful, and as she followed her aunt downstairs into the great hall where the first of the guests were arriving, she thought, *I don't belong here.*

She had to admit as she looked round the room, that they had made a good job of the decorations and the place looked very festive. The musicians hired for the occasion were tuning their instruments and the guests, shaking off the prevailing gloom engendered by the long drawn-out war, moved around the hall, chattering like magpies.

Sir Thomas leaned on his cane, greeting each one as they came through the door, while the butler, who should have retired long since, crept around on bowed legs, a tray balanced precariously, offering drinks.

Ada stood by Sir Thomas's side, acting the hostess and loving every minute, Tilly thought with a wry smile. She recognised some of the faces and her smile deepened as she spotted the mayor of Lydmouth talking to the Vicar and reflected on her aunt's injunction not to mention the forge. How often had she helped her father to shoe their horses, as well as doing other smithing jobs for their households?

She glanced down at the blue satin gown her aunt had had made for the occasion and thought it quite possible they wouldn't recognise the black-smith's daughter in her new guise. She resolved to behave as unobtrusively as possible and, when the band struck up for the first dance, she retreated to a window seat and sat half-hidden by the velvet drapes.

Tapping her feet in time to the music she gradually relaxed. No one was taking any notice of her. Her aunt was engrossed in conversation with the mayor's wife and, to Tilly's relief, seemed to have forgotten that she had vowed to introduce her niece to some 'suitable young people.'

A voice in her ear startled her and she turned to see Richard Lacey holding two glasses. 'It's rather warm in here, Miss Masters. I thought you might like a refreshing drink.'

'Thank you, sir,' she replied, taking

the glass. She sipped cautiously, giggling as bubbles went up her nose.

'I don't suppose you've had champagne before,' Richard observed.

'No — and I'm not sure I like it. Cider's more to my taste.'

'You'll get used to it. Have some more.'

'No thank you, sir.' Tilly hadn't realised how thirsty she was and had finished the glass almost without thinking. Now, she felt even warmer and her head felt a little fuzzy too. She needed some fresh air. Standing up, she tried to walk away. 'I think my aunt is looking for me,' she murmured.

Richard laughed. 'Your aunt is engrossed in her conversation. Why don't you dance with me?' He took the glass from her and set it on the window seat, then took her hand and led her onto the dance floor.

Tilly tried to protest. 'I am really not a good dancer, sir. Besides, I don't know this music.'

'Nonsense. I am sure you've danced

with the village lads at harvest suppers and such. This is no different.' He grasped her firmly around the waist and whirled her around.

After a minute or two her ears adjusted to the rhythm of the music and she found she was able to follow Richard's lead, although occasionally her feet betrayed her and she almost stumbled. But he kept hold of her and smiled down at her. Soon, she found she was enjoying herself and she gave herself up to the music. If only she were dancing with Nathan, she would be perfectly happy, she thought — only to be struck by the thought that she had never danced with her sweetheart.

As Richard had guessed, she had gone to harvest suppers and village socials, doing the old-fashioned country dances she had learned as a child. But she had never danced like this; never been held closely in Nathan's arms, felt his breath on her cheek or his hand firm in the small of her back.

She gave a little gasp and stepped

back, breaking the rhythm of the dance and stumbling a little.

'I'm sorry. Did I step on your foot?' Richard asked, smiling down at her. 'Perhaps we had better sit down.' He led her back to her seat and sat down beside her, uncomfortably close.

She tried to move away but he pulled her closer. She felt his breath on her cheek. 'You know, when I saw you sitting here, I scarcely recognised you. I wondered who the beautiful young lady could be.' He put his hand under her chin and tilted her face up, gazing into her eyes. 'Surely a fairy godmother has waved her magic wand.' He laughed and Tilly felt herself blushing much against her will.

'No fairy godmother. This was my aunt's doing.' She pulled away and smoothed her skirt. 'This is not the real me, Mr Lacey. I am much more at home in the smithy.'

'It's true, you do seem to be competent at the work but it really is no life for a young lady. I am sure, if your mother were here, she would agree with your aunt. I can't imagine what your father is thinking of, allowing you to act as his assistant.'

Tilly stood up, her face flaming. 'And I cannot imagine what business it is of yours. My father needs me, and until his assistant returns from the war I shall continue to work with him.'

'Miss Masters — Tilly — I did not mean . . .'

But Tilly did not stay to hear his apology. She swept out of the room and ran up the stairs to the little room where she had left her everyday clothes. Tearing off the satin gown, she threw herself down on the little truckle bed and let the tears come.

Why did Richard Lacey have to spoil her evening? She had been enjoying herself up until he had made his remarks about her work. Why did everyone think they knew what was best for her?

She knew she shouldn't get upset. She should be used to it by now —

being told it was no life for a young girl. Even Nathan had hinted that she wasn't needed at the forge when he first came to work there. But gradually, he had come to respect her dedication, to realise that she had a natural aptitude for blacksmithing. And indeed, their love had grown out of that very mutual respect.

Thinking of Nathan brought a fresh burst of tears as she recalled her words to Richard Lacey — that she would continue to work at the smithy until his return. For the first time her confidence wavered and she allowed the thought that he might not come back to enter her mind. What would she do then? Would she be happy working as a blacksmith without him at her side to share the work?

4

Nathan was tired — not just physically weary but mentally exhausted. Would the carnage never end? He and Ginger trudged along behind the cart, not speaking, their eyes fixed on the ground, trying to avoid stumbling on the debris poking up through the mud. Among the shards of wood and metal were dead men and horses, victims of the last great bombardment.

Nathan tried not to think about it, instead re-playing in his head the comparatively light-hearted moment he and Ginger had shared yesterday evening. The cry of 'mail ho' had set his heart racing in anticipation. Tearing open the parcel and savouring its contents had lifted his spirits for a while. It didn't matter that the socks Tilly had knitted were mis-matched and misshapen. He knew they had been made with love. Holding them up in the flickering candlelight of the dugout, he and Ginger had grinned at each other. The letter that had come with the parcel was a more private affair and he had waited until he was alone to read it. Now it nestled close to his heart tucked safely in the pocket of his battle dress.

Now it was back to the real world and, although it was quiet for the moment, Nathan knew that the guns could start up again at any time. They had been sent forward to rescue as many horses as they could, many injured but even more simply bogged down in the viscous mud and in danger of drowning.

Those beyond help were loaded onto the carts. He had an inkling what would happen to the carcasses back at camp but he tried not to think about it, focusing instead on what he could do to help those animals that were not too badly injured. In the months he'd been out here he had learned a lot, his work on the farm before he had gone to work for Ben Masters standing him in good stead.

'You've got a way with horses,' the veterinary officer had said. 'Leave the farriery to the others. I need you to assist me with the wounded.'

Nathan no longer thought it strange that the men of the veterinary detachment gave more thought to the animals in their care than to the men. Horses were vital out here, and with so many being killed, they had to do their best to patch up the injured animals and make them fit for battle again.

The barrage had started up again almost unnoticed but an almost human scream, heard even over the sound of the guns, jerked him out of his reverie. 'Come on, Ginger. There's another one over there.' He left the road, stumbling towards a shell hole. The stretcher bearers were already there, lifting wounded men and carrying them to a waiting ambulance.

They scarcely glanced at the horse which was beginning to writhe in its death throes, caught in the traces which still attached it the gun carriage it had been pulling. Its companion had already succumbed to its wounds and was slowly sinking into the mire.

The plunging hooves were hampering the efforts of the stretcher bearers. 'Get that animal out of here,' one of them snapped at Nathan.

'Doing me best, mate,' he muttered, sliding down into the shell hole up to his knees in mud. The poor horses were even more terrified of the constant noise than he was. He couldn't deny he was scared but concern for the animals he loved went some way towards holding the threatened panic at bay. He caught hold of the mare's bridle, trying to soothe it. 'I'll hold her, Ginger. Do what you can.'

'Nothing to do — just put her out of her misery.'

'Let's get it over with then.' Nathan stroked the animal's nose, blowing softly into its nostrils and murmuring in its ear. As he wiped the mud away, he saw the white blaze and recognised the mare whose wound he had dressed only a few days before. A lump came to his throat. *What a waste,* he thought, as he put his pistol to the mare's temple.

Ginger stumbled to stand up, waving to the men with the cart. 'Load this one up,' he called.

Nathan was still holding the mare's head, struggling to hold back his tears. Why, out of all the hundreds of animals he had looked after, had this one got to him? He raised his head as Ginger's voice penetrated his thoughts. 'Come on, mate. We ain't done yet.'

He dashed his hand across his eyes and started to get up. But as he got to his feet, a blast of hot air lifted him and threw him back into the shell hole. Gobs of mud and who knew what else rained down and a deathly silence enveloped him. He shook his head.

Gradually, over the ringing in his ears, faint cries and the shrill neighing of a horse came to him.

He tried to stand, but a searing pain

shot through his leg and he flopped back into the mud. He couldn't see very well either, and he raised his hand to his forehead. It came away wet and he saw that it was streaked with blood, although as yet he could feel no pain.

The horse's whinnying had quietened and Nathan thought it must have died. He managed to drag himself free of the clinging mud and pull himself to the edge of the hole, wincing as the pain in his leg intensified. There was no sign of Ginger but he could hear moaning. 'Ginge, you all right, mate?'

But it wasn't Ginger and Nathan swallowed hard as he realised his friend had taken the brunt of the blast and was beyond help. A little further away, Captain Weston lay tangled in the reins and stirrups of his horse.

'I'm coming, sir,' he called.

'No, Miller, stay where you are. Keep your head down.'

'Can't leave you there, sir,' Nathan muttered and began to crawl towards the wounded officer.

As he crawled, the ringing in his ears abated and he became aware that the barrage was still going on. He wasn't sure if it was the ground shaking or his own body trembling but he carried on. By the time he had reached Captain Weston, the horse had ceased its struggles but the officer was still trapped beneath it.

Nathan pulled his knife out of its sheath and cut through the tangled leather reins. Gritting his teeth against the pain in his leg, he shoved against the horse's body and managed to shift it enough to pull the officer free.

'Thanks, Miller,' Captain Weston gasped, reaching out a hand.

As Nathan grasped it, the captain gave a little sigh and lost consciousness. Away from the dubious protection of the shell hole, the noise of the barrage was even louder and Nathan knew he had to get to safety.

He never knew how long it took to crawl those few yards, dragging Captain Weston behind him. Reaching the shell hole, he gave a last heave and pushed the wounded man over the edge and was about to fall in beside him when another explosion rent the air.

★   ★   ★

After the ball, Tilly had resisted her aunt's pleas to stay in Lydmouth and returned home. She had to admit she had enjoyed the brief respite from the hard life of the forge, and she had even enjoyed dancing with Richard Lacey. But once she was back working alongside her father she realised that this was where she belonged.

Despite there still being no more word from Nathan, she tried hard to convince herself that he was all right. Hadn't he said he was working with the horses behind the lines? What could happen to him there?

An iron frost had the countryside in its grip and Tilly was glad of the heat from the forge. She had to go outside for more coal, though, and she shivered as she trundled the wheelbarrow round to the store. Shovelling the coal into the barrow soon warmed her up and she paused to loosen her shawl, glancing across the village green as she saw the carrier's cart stopping outside the post office.

A figure climbed down and Tilly's heart sank. Surely Aunt Ada wasn't paying another visit? Didn't she realise that Tilly didn't have time to play hostess over the best tea cups?

But as the woman crossed the green she realised it was not her aunt. The small stooped figure hugged her shawl across her bosom, her steps faltering as she saw Tilly standing by the smithy.

Tilly had never met Nathan's mother, but somehow she knew who it was and her heart began to hammer. There was only one reason Mrs Miller would come to Lydford. She dropped the handles of the wheelbarrow and took a few hesitant steps towards the visitor. 'Nathan?' Her mouth was dry and the word came out as a whisper.

'You're Tilly, aren't you, me dear? I recognised you from my boy's description.' She gave a sad smile. 'He said you were a pretty lass.'

Although Tilly knew what she was going to say, she had to ask. 'Is he all right? Please say he's just wounded, not . . . ?'

'I got a telegram. *Missing,* it says.'

Tilly's legs felt weak and she thought she would fall, but she steeled herself and managed to say, 'Thank you for coming to tell me. You must be tired and cold after coming all this way. Shall we go inside and I'll make you a hot drink?'

'That's kind of you, lass.'

'I'll just speak to my father then.' She took the coal into the smithy, amazed at how calm she sounded. 'Pa, Nathan's mother is here. Can you get on by yourself for a while?'

'What does she want?' Ben asked, without interrupting the strokes with the hammer. Then, as the realisation dawned on him, he dropped the bar he

95

was working on and clapped a hand to his forehead. 'Nathan. She has news of the lad?'

Tilly nodded, blinking hard to hold back tears, and he took her hand. 'Not good news, then?'

'He's missing, Pa, not . . . '

'There's hope, then. Well, lass, better get in the house and look after Mrs Miller. Take your time. I'll join you when I'm done.'

Inside the cottage Tilly stoked the range and sat Nathan's mother in the one armchair close to the fire. There were so many questions she wanted to ask but she could see that Mrs Miller was in no state to talk. She must have got frozen travelling over from Wendon in the carrier's cart, as well as seeming to be still in a state of shock from the news.

Tilly busied herself at the range to give Mrs Miller time to recover as well as to hide her own threatening tears. She poured the tea and thrust the cup into the older woman's hands. 'There, that'll warm you up,' she said with an attempt at a smile. She couldn't let herself cry in front of Nathan's mother.

The older woman gulped the tea, clasping her hands round the cup for warmth. 'That's better. Thank you, lass.' She put the cup down, her hand shaking a little.

'You shouldn't have come all that way in this weather,' Tilly said.

'I had to, me dear. I promised Nathan I'd let you know if . . . ' Her voice faltered but she quickly composed herself. 'It only says 'missing'. That means there's hope, doesn't it?'

'Of course it does,' Tilly said quickly. 'They would say if . . . ' But her own voice tailed off then and the two women sat in silence for a few minutes, gazing into the flames of the kitchen range, each lost in their own thoughts.

At last Mrs Miller stood up, adjusting her shawl. 'I'd better go, Tilly. The carrier won't wait and I must get back to Wendon. It'll be dark soon and I've got to shut the chickens up. Don't want that old fox to get them.'

'I'll walk across the green with you,' Tilly offered. Her mind was teeming with questions but she knew there would be no answers. The official telegrams left only the barest flicker of hope in their stark message.

As Nathan's mother climbed up into the cart, Tilly reached out and patted her arm. 'He will come back — I'm sure of it,' she said.

Mrs Miller squeezed her hand and mustered a small, tight smile. 'We'll pray it is so, lass.'

The carter whipped up his old nag and Tilly stood in the gathering dusk watching until they were out of sight. Only then did the tears begin to fall. For, in spite of her brave words, she didn't really believe them. Too many young men had been reported missing over the past few years, only to have it confirmed months later that they had not survived.

5

Spring had arrived at last but Tilly was beginning to feel that it would always be winter in her heart. For weeks after Mrs Miller's visit she watched anxiously for any news, her stomach churning until the post boy had passed by the smithy. Of course, any official letter would go to Nathan's mother, but Mrs Miller had promised to let Tilly know as soon as she heard anything.

Whenever the carrier's cart stopped outside the Post Office she found herself glancing up and staring across the village green to see if he was carrying a passenger.

The only visitor during this dreadful time was Aunt Ada and Tilly braced herself for yet another argument. But, to her relief, her aunt seemed to have abandoned her campaign to try and persuade her to live in town.

'I can see you're happy in your work, my dear,' she said, as she sat at the table on a fine spring morning, sipping daintily from the best china. 'Besides, while this war continues, we women must do our bit.'

'That's what I keep telling you, aunt,' Tilly replied, privately thinking that the war had nothing to do with it.

'Well, they say it should all be over soon. They've got this new man in charge now — supreme commander they call him. I read it in the paper.'

Tilly didn't reply. She had almost given up following news of the war. What did it matter if a few more miles of ground had been taken if it meant the deaths of so many men? What was it all for? Hadn't they already fought one battle over this same stretch of ground only a couple of years ago?

Ada got up. 'It's no use moping, girl. That young man was no good to you anyway.'

'You're talking as if he's dead. He's not — I don't believe it. We'd have heard if he . . . ' Tilly started to sob.

Ada patted her shoulder awkwardly. 'I didn't mean that. I know you haven't given up hope. But I'm worried about you, girl. You're not eating. Just look at you — thin as a rake. Your pa's worried too.'

Tilly blew her nose and looked up. 'I don't want Pa upset. He does depend on me you know.'

'Yes, of course he does. But the war will soon be over and you'll have to start thinking about the future. I don't want you making the same mistake your mother did.'

As usual when her aunt seemed to be criticising her parents, Tilly's temper erupted. 'Marrying Pa wasn't a mistake as you call it,' she snapped. 'They were happy — they loved each other. That's more important than a posh house and servants and . . . ' Her voice broke.

Ada's voice softened. 'I do know how you feel, dear, believe me. But as you get older things change. I just want the best for you.'

Regretting her outburst, Tilly sniffed and tried to smile. 'I know, Aunt. But what you think is best isn't necessarily what I want.'

Ada adjusted her bonnet in the mirror over the range. 'We'll see. Just so you know, my dear, that I'm always there if you need anything.'

As Tilly watched her striding along the path across the green, head high and shoulders back, she couldn't help feeling a surge of affection for the older woman. Maybe she really did feel that she was offering her a better life, but she'd never convince Tilly otherwise. Still, she reflected, although she loved her work in the forge, she had to admit that these days it didn't have quite the same allure as it had when she was working alongside Nathan.

When the tears threatened again, she too squared her shoulders. She wouldn't cry any more — because he was coming back one day, she knew it.

★ ★ ★

As the spring turned to summer, Tilly threw herself into work, and if it hadn't been for her father and the need to prepare his meals, she probably wouldn't have rested at all. She was thankful that the forge remained busy, the fire never allowed to go out as a constant stream of farmers, carters and villagers turned up at the door of the smithy. The war might still be raging over in Europe but here, in their corner of rural Sussex, the work of the local farmers seemed more important. There were harrows and plough shares to mend, scythes needed sharpening or fitting with new blades, and the few remaining cart horses had to be shoed, not to mention the village housewives needing a new handle for a pan or a set of fire tongs repaired.

Occasionally, one of their customers would ask for news of Nathan, and Tilly would shake her head, leaving her father to do the talking. It was becoming harder to hold on to the hope that he had been wounded or captured.

Surely they would have heard if that were so.

One fine June day as Tilly was helping her father and the wheelwright to fix the iron tyre on to a cartwheel, she heard a horse trotting up the lane. She forced herself not to look up, feeling sure that it was Richard Lacey. He had ridden over from Lydsey Manor several times since the New Year ball, usually with the excuse that his horse needed attending to.

Tilly kept her eyes on the lump of metal in the fire, waiting for her father to nod when it was ready to pull out. She told herself it was the heat of the forge which had caused the flush to her cheeks. She would not acknowledge how disturbing she found his quizzical smile, his compliments on the quality of her work.

The visitor dismounted and a shadow fell across the doorway.

Ben looked up. 'Can I help you, sir?'

'Is this the home of Miss Tilly Masters?' a strange voice asked.

She glanced up to see an officer of the Sussex Regiment standing awkwardly and twisting his cap in his hands.

'And what do you want with my daughter?' Ben asked.

Before he could reply, Tilly dropped the tongs with a clatter and whirled round. 'It's Nathan — you have news?'

Hope died as she took in the officer's expression, the tightening of his lips, the shadow across his eyes.

'Regrettably so, Miss Masters. You must prepare yourself . . . '

'But the telegram said he was missing . . . '

'I was there.' He paused. 'Sergeant Miller saved my life but, in doing so, I fear he sacrificed his own.'

Tilly felt faint and her legs threatened to give way. Her father put his arm round her shoulder. 'Bear up, lass, bear up.' He turned to the officer. 'I think we knew deep down, sir. But thank you for coming in person.'

'It's the least I could do. I thought

you might like to hear the full story. I have already visited Sergeant Miller's mother and she told me of his affection for your daughter — and his respect for you as his employer.'

'We appreciate it, sir — don't we, Tilly?' Ben gave her shoulder a reassuring squeeze.

With a great effort she pulled herself together and nodded. 'Can we offer you some refreshment, sir?'

'Thank you — something cold? It was a warm ride from Wendon.'

'Come into the cottage and sit down. Pa will see to your horse.'

As the man followed her into the kitchen, Tilly noticed that he was limping. He lowered himself carefully into a chair, laying his peaked cap on the table in front of him and looking about him. 'Sergeant Miller often talked about the forge and this cottage. He was happy working here.'

'If he was so happy, why did he have to go and join the army before he needed to?' Tilly couldn't keep the break from showing in her voice, or the faint hint of bitterness.

'He was doing his duty — as we all are,' the man replied.

'Duty,' Tilly muttered under her breath as she poured cider from a jug into a pewter mug and set it down in front of him. He picked it up and took a long draught.

'I do understand how you feel, Miss Masters,' he said, putting the mug down. 'I beg your pardon. I haven't introduced myself. My name is James Weston — Captain Weston. Sergeant Miller looked after my horse. He was a good man — well respected by his fellows.' He paused and took another drink. 'A brave man, too.'

'What happened? Are you quite sure . . . ?' Tilly couldn't stop the tears welling up.

'There can be little doubt, I'm afraid.' Captain Weston paused. 'It was all so confusing — the noise, the mud . . . ' He shook his head. 'I thought I was done for. I was pinned down under my horse — I couldn't move. But

Sergeant Miller crawled towards me. How he shifted that great beast on his own I'll never know. But he pulled me away and dragged me to safety.'

Tilly was about to speak but the officer seemed to have forgotten she was there. His eyes had glazed over as if he was seeing something other than the homely cottage kitchen. After a few moments he gave a shudder and looked up. 'I lost consciousness, woke up in the dressing station. I asked about the sergeant but no one could tell me anything. Then the stretcher bearer who had brought me in said that there was no sign of a sergeant anywhere near the spot where it had happened. They found the remains of his friend though, so the only explanation seemed to be that he had been killed, too.'

'But they told us missing — not killed,' Tilly repeated, still unwilling to give up hope entirely.

'The official view is that we tell the relatives that, unless there is no doubt at all.' He stood up and picked up his cap. 'I am so sorry to be the one to bring such news.'

He limped outside and untied the bridle of his horse. As he mounted, he looked down at Tilly. 'Nathan Miller was a good man,' he said with emotion, and spurred the animal into a trot.

As he rode away down the lane, Tilly stood looking after him, her fists clenched at her sides. 'He said 'was',' she muttered. 'But I say he *is* a good man.' She turned back to the smithy and went inside, picked up the tongs and resumed the task which Captain Weston had interrupted.

As she thrust the bar of iron into the flames, her father said, 'Everything all right, lass?'

'No, Pa, it is not all right.' She shook her head. 'I don't care what he says — he didn't see Nathan after he was rescued. How does he know he was really dead? I won't believe it — I won't — not till someone gives me proof.'

Ben shook his head too. 'Oh, lass,' he murmured.

6

Ben looked up from his breakfast as Tilly re-entered the cottage. She had rushed outside on hearing the post boy's bicycle clattering up the lane and had been gone for a few minutes. 'No news, then?' he asked.

'Just a note from Mrs Miller. She's heard nothing else since Captain Weston's visit.'

'Nothing official, you mean?'

'That's good, isn't it, Pa? If they were sure they'd let her know, surely?'

Ben laid down his knife and fork and shook his head. 'I know you won't give up, but you heard what the captain said. You can't spend the rest of your life grieving — or living on false hope. You have to move on.'

Tilly guessed he was thinking as much of himself as anything. She remembered how he had been after her mother died and she knew that, however much he tried to hide it, he still missed her.

'I don't think I can, Pa,' she said.

Ben pushed his plate away and stood up. 'But you must, lass. You're still so young . . . '

Tilly stood up and began to clear the table, her shoulders hunched as she stood at the sink swilling the plates under the stream of water from the pump. She clattered the things into the enamel bowl and poured hot water from the kettle, swilling the washing soda around to dissolve it.

She heard Ben sigh and kept her back to him until she heard him leave the room and stride across the yard. Soon, the sound of hammer on iron reached her ears and she knew that, as she herself so often did, he was venting his feelings in physical labour.

Things were quiet in the forge today and Tilly was grateful that she could avoid her father's attempts to cheer her up. His meaningless remarks were intended as comfort and she didn't want to lose her temper with him.

She had already done the week's wash before breakfast and now she took the basket of dripping wet things out to the mangle which stood in a corner of the yard. It was hard work manhandling the heavy sheets through the rollers and her arms were aching long before she had finished.

As she bent to lift another sheet out of the basket, a voice said, 'Do you need a hand with that?'

She straightened up and couldn't help laughing when she saw who it was. 'Mr Lacey, I hardly think this is the kind of work for a gentleman.'

'Why not? I can see that it would be far easier for you with another pair of hands to assist.'

She hesitated, still not sure if he was teasing her. But he already had his hands on the handle and, as she fed the sheet between the rollers he began to turn it. She had to admit it was a lot easier and she remembered as a child helping her mother with this same task and her laughing voice saying, 'Many hands make light work.'

The job was soon done and she turned to Richard Lacey with a smile. 'Thank you, kind sir.' She picked up the laundry basket and started round the side of the cottage towards the orchard.

He followed her, and began to help her peg the washing on the line stretched between two apple trees. She couldn't help laughing. No man in the village would lower himself to help a woman with her household chores. 'I can manage, you know. I'm sure you didn't come all the way over to Lydford just to help me with the laundry.'

Richard laughed too. 'Not entirely.'

'And I don't believe that your horse has cast another shoe already.' She gestured toward the beautiful black stallion which was tethered to the rail outside the smithy.

'Not this time. I have another little job for you. The latch on one of the park gates has worn and I wondered if your father — or you — could make a new one. It is not an urgent job, if you are busy. I can leave it with you and come back another day.'

Tilly bit back a smile. She wasn't a vain girl but she wasn't so naïve that she hadn't realised Richard's frequent visits to the smithy were just excuses to see her and to flirt a little. His interest in her wasn't serious — it couldn't be, given their different stations in life. But even if it was, she could not respond to him — not while her heart still belonged to Nathan. At the thought a shadow passed across her face and she felt guilty for enjoying another man's company, innocent as it was.

Richard stopped smiling and took her hand. 'I take it there has been no news of Sergeant Miller, then? I saw his mother in the village. The poor woman is quite broken up.'

'I had a letter from her this morning. She says she has not given up hope — not while there is no official confirmation of his death.' Tilly's voice faltered on the last word and Richard's grip on her hand tightened.

'I know you and your father must miss him sorely. But, Miss Masters — Tilly — life goes on, you know. My own brother . . . ' Now his voice faltered and Tilly gazed up at him compassionately.

'My aunt told me — I was so sorry to hear the news. Your poor father.'

Richard still had hold of her hand. 'Don't look so sad, Tilly. I'd give anything to see you smile again. Remember the night of the ball? We have to think of the good times.'

Before she could reply, they were interrupted by the sound of horses neighing, angry shouts, followed by a scream of agony. Snatching her hand away from Richard's, Tilly rushed into the yard.

Richard's stallion, still tethered beside the smithy, reared and plunged as a huge carthorse galloped past her and out into the lane with Farmer Johnson chasing after it.

A young lad, his face chalk white,

scrambled to his feet, gabbling incoherently. But Tilly only had eyes for her father who lay on the dusty ground, groaning.

She threw herself down beside him. 'Pa! Are you all right?' She stroked his pale face as his eyes rolled up in his head and he lost consciousness. She looked up at the farmer's lad. 'What happened?'

'It were old Blossom,' the boy gasped. 'She went mad — kicked out with her hind legs. Master Ben pushed me out of the way just in time. But Blossom caught him in the chest, knocked him down.' The lad was shaking. 'He'll be all right, won't he?'

Tilly shook her head, taking her father's hand and murmuring to him. But his eyes were closed and he didn't seem to hear her.

Richard had succeeded in calming his own horse and now knelt beside her, running his hands over Ben's body to determine his injuries. 'Looks like a couple of broken ribs,' he announced. 'I think we'd better get him into his own bed. Tilly, get some bandages, any old strips of cloth will do. We must bind his ribs to stop any movement.'

As Tilly rushed off to do his bidding, he turned to the farmer's lad. 'Here, boy, what's your name?'

'Jimmy, sir.' The boy was still shaking.

'Well, Jimmy, I need a hand here. Kneel beside me and take the bandages when Tilly brings them. I'm going to lift him and, when I tell you to, I need you to slide the bandages underneath him.'

Having something to do seemed to calm the lad. By the time Tilly returned with some strips of old sheet, they had torn open Ben's shirt to reveal a massive bruise. But it wasn't this that made Tilly gasp. In the centre of his chest, a sliver of bone protruded from a bleeding, jagged wound.

'Oh, Pa,' she sobbed, dropping to her knees beside him.

'Don't distress yourself, Tilly. I'm sure he'll be all right. We just need to bind this tightly — otherwise the bone could pierce his lung. It looks clean enough so there shouldn't be any infection.'

Richard patted her arm in reassurance. Then, with Tilly and Jimmy helping, he proceeded to bind Ben's ribs.

The clatter of hooves in the yard heralded the return of Farmer Johnson, red-faced and sweating, leading his horse by its bridle. He tied the animal securely before coming across the yard and looking down at the group.

'I don't know what got into the brute,' he said. 'She's never behaved like that before — usually a gentle old soul.' He gestured at the blacksmith's prostrate form. 'That could be young Jimmy lying there, you know. Ben pushed the lad out of the way. I hope to God he's going to be all right.'

'We've done all we can for the moment. Now we need to get him into the house.' Richard turned to Tilly. 'I don't think we can get him upstairs. Is there somewhere he can lie down?'

'There's the sofa in the parlour. We don't use it much. I'll get some sheets and a pillow and make up a bed for him there.' Reluctantly, she let go of her father's hand and hurried into the cottage, determined not to cry.

When she came back, Richard and the farmer had lifted Ben onto a hurdle. They carried him into the cottage and gently transferred him to the horsehair sofa. Tilly immediately covered him with a blanket and stood for a moment gazing down at his ashen face. His eyes were still closed and he hadn't moved.

She turned round when she felt Richard's hand on her shoulder. 'I've sent young Jimmy for the doctor,' he said. 'I'll stay with you till he comes.'

'There's no need,' she replied.

'Very well.' He shrugged his shoulders and left the room.

Tilly pulled a stool close to the sofa and sat down, taking her father's hand. She smoothed back the sparse wisps of hair from his forehead, noting his laboured breathing. Had the broken bone pierced the lung? How did Richard know? He wasn't a doctor. She got up and paced the room. Why was the doctor taking so long? He should be here by now. She turned back to her father. 'Pa, please get better. What shall I do if . . . ?'

As if in reply, Ben stirred and moaned, but his eyes remained closed. His face had regained a little colour but beads of sweat had formed on his brow. It was very hot in the small room and Tilly went to the window and opened it a little. She heard voices from the yard and realised that Richard was still here, talking to Farmer Johnson.

What had made the horse kick out like that? Had the boy been holding her firmly enough? He was only a little lad. *If only I'd been there to help,* she thought. A wave of guilt swept over her as she recalled that only moments before the accident she had actually been laughing and joking with Richard in the orchard.

She turned away from the window as the sound of the doctor's car — the first and only one in the locality — reached her ears. She ran outside as he stopped his vehicle and climbed down from the high seat, grabbing his black bag and striding towards the cottage.

'The lad told me what happened. Where is the patient?' he demanded.

'He's in the parlour.' Tilly showed him to the stuffy little room which had hardly been used since her mother died, not even when Aunt Ada visited.

The doctor put his bag on the small table and pulled back the blanket. 'You'd better wait outside. I'll call you when I've examined him,' he said.

Reluctantly, Tilly left the room and wandered out to the yard, where Richard was still talking to Mr Johnson.

'I thought you'd gone,' she said.

'We felt it only right to wait and hear what the doctor's verdict was,' Richard replied.

'Aye, lass. I feel it were my fault. Old Blossom hasn't been herself for a while.

I put it down to the heat,' Mr Johnson said. 'But she were limping a bit so I thought her shoe might be loose. She wouldn't let me look, so I brought her along to your pa.'

'You mustn't blame yourself, Mr Johnson.' Tilly looked at the old carthorse, now as docile as usual. 'Would you like me to look at her?'

'No.' Richard and the farmer spoke in unison. The farmer's face coloured. 'Sorry, lass — it's just that I wouldn't forgive myself if anything else were to happen.'

'I don't think it would be wise, Tilly,' Richard agreed.

'You can't let the poor horse limp all the way back to the farm,' Tilly protested. 'Besides, she seems calm enough now. And if you both hold her, she should be all right.'

'All right, lass — if Mr Lacey will lend a hand,' the farmer suggested. 'And you, Jimmy, keep out of the way.'

'I still think you should get the vet to look at her,' Richard muttered. But he went to the horse's head and took a firm grip on her bridle, stroking her nose and talking quietly. Farmer Johnson stood to one side, his hand firmly on the animal's hind quarters.

As Tilly approached, Blossom's ears went back and she snickered. But the two men held on firmly and Tilly gently took hold of the hind leg, lifting the hoof off the ground. Parting the feathery fringe which hung over Blossom's hoof, she could see straight away what the problem was. A large thorn protruded from the animal's hock almost hidden by the tangled hair. Ben must have unwittingly touched it when he started work on the shoe.

If only Nathan were here, Tilly thought. *He'd know exactly what to do.* He'd always had a way with horses. She closed her eyes momentarily, conjuring up his image, remembering how she had loved watching him work. 'Gentle, but firm,' she murmured, echoing his words.

Grasping the thorn in the pincers,

she pulled it free, releasing a stream of infected matter. She stepped back, letting go of Blossom's leg. 'There,' she said, holding up the offending three-inch spike. 'No wonder she was upset.'

Farmer Johnson drew a hand across his forehead. 'Why didn't I see that?' He stroked the horse's nose. 'Well, me old beauty, what a lot of bother we've caused.' He turned to Tilly. 'I hope your old pa will be all right. I feel real bad about all this.'

Tilly didn't know what to say and busied herself bathing the wound. 'I think you should get the vet to take a look,' she said. 'It's infected.'

Farmer Johnson nodded. 'I'll get him to call,' he said.

As Tilly finished bandaging the horse's leg, the doctor emerged from the cottage and crossed the yard towards them. 'I've done the best I can for the moment. He should be in hospital, but I am reluctant to move him.'

'Will he be all right?' Tilly asked.

'I really can't say just now. Mr Lacey did a good job of first aid. If there is no infection, your father should heal in time. He has a strong constitution so ... ' He paused. 'Just keep him immobile, bathe the wound frequently, give him nourishing soups and broths. I'll come back in a day or two to see how he's coming along.' He threw his bag onto the passenger seat and climbed up into the car.

In the silence that followed, Richard said. 'Will you manage all right? Would you like me to fetch your aunt?'

'No, thank you. I'll be fine. Let's leave it for a day or two — I'm sure Pa will be up and around in no time. I can look after him.'

'Very well.' He untethered his horse and mounted, leaning down to take her hand. 'I'll call in a day or two to see how he is.'

Farmer Johnson led Blossom out into the lane, once more apologising for the trouble he'd caused. He pressed a few coins into Tilly's hand. 'There, lass, that'll keep you going till your pa's fit for work again.'

'That's far too much, Mr Johnson,' she protested.

'Take it, lass. It's small compensation for what happened.'

Tilly tucked the money into her apron pocket, thanked him and hurried back into the cottage, biting back a sob when she saw that her father had still not regained consciousness.

7

Tilly tipped a bucketful of coal on to the forge bed and raked it towards the middle, then started up the bellows. When the coals were glowing, she took the straight bar of iron and thrust it into the flames. She worked quickly and efficiently, shaping the bar into a loop to go over a gatepost. It was an urgent job as the gate had blown down in a recent gale and the rusted fastener had snapped.

Farmer Johnson had told her the sheep had strayed into the next field and what a job he'd had to round them up. 'I've tied it up with string but it needs a proper fastener,' he said.

Tilly had promised to have it ready that morning. It was still early, but already she was exhausted. She glanced across at the bench where the latch that Richard had brought her on the day of her father's accident still lay. There had been no time to work on it and he had not mentioned it, confirming her belief that asking her to do the repair had just been an excuse to visit the smithy.

Her face flamed and guilt gnawed at her as she recalled how she had light-heartedly flirted with him on that sunny morning three weeks ago. Determinedly, she put Richard Lacey out of her mind and concentrated on the job she was doing. She had to keep going, however tired she was.

Ben was still bed-ridden and didn't seem to be recovering as fast as the doctor had predicted. Despite her care in keeping it clean, the wound where the broken bone had punctured his skin had become inflamed. Ben was in constant pain and, in his delirium, he often confused Tilly with Mary, his long-dead wife.

Between tending to her father and trying to keep the forge going, Tilly had little time to grieve for Nathan or to question Richard's attentions.

Despite the fact that he was supposed to be running his father's estate, Richard always seemed to have time to ride over to Lydford to enquire after Ben's welfare, often bringing gifts of fruit from the hot houses at the Manor. He had also helped to bring Ben's bed downstairs and set it up in the parlour for her.

'More comfortable than that old sofa,' he said, 'and it'll save you having to keep going upstairs to see to him.'

Tilly had smiled gratefully if a little warily. She found it hard to believe that he was being so helpful out of the goodness of his heart.

Aunt Ada had visited too, but seldom stayed to be of any practical help. Her solution to the problems brought about by Ben's accident was the usual one. Ben should be in hospital and Tilly should shut up the smithy and go to stay with her in town.

As she straightened up and rubbed her aching back, Tilly could almost agree with her. But the forge was Ben's life and she knew that, even if she closed down for only a matter of weeks, people would take their custom elsewhere. When he was better, it would be hard to recover that business.

And he must get better, Tilly thought. She'd lost Nathan; she couldn't bear to lose her father also.

She worked on for another hour or so, determinedly trying to put her worries to the back of her mind. Pa was relying on her to keep things going and she would not disappoint him.

But although she loved her work, delighting in seeing the different shapes emerging from the molten metal, taking pride and satisfaction in a job well done, today it all seemed too much. She was bone weary. The long hours of work with no assistance, as well as trying to keep the cottage clean and looking after her father, were taking their toll.

She plunged the hot iron into the bucket of water, gave the finished implement a half-hearted polish, and glanced across at the pile of broken and rusty tools that waited her attention. She really ought to start on the next job. But first she'd check on Pa, see if he needed anything.

Outside, she stretched and looked up into a clear blue sky. It was a glorious day. Summer had crept up on her almost unnoticed, the days passing in a blur of exhaustion. She took a moment to savour the fresh air, the scent of the roses scrambling round the cottage door, before going in to the cool dark interior.

She stirred the range into life and filled the kettle from the pump before opening the door to the parlour. She saw immediately that Ben was no better. The covers were rumpled and thrust to one side, and her father's face was flushed, the sparse strands of his hair clinging to his scalp, damp with sweat.

She hurried across to the bedside and knelt beside him. 'Pa, are you all right?' she whispered, stroking his forehead.

Ben's head moved restlessly from side to side and he muttered something indistinguishable.

'What is it, Pa? Can I get you anything?'

He plucked at the sheet, continuing to mutter softly.

Tilly choked back a sob. Last time the doctor called he had reassured her that her father was on the mend. She had followed his instructions faithfully but, despite her efforts, today he seemed worse than ever.

She got to her feet and went into the other room to fetch water and a cloth. She held a glass to Ben's lips and tried to urge him to drink but most of it dribbled down his neck. She wiped it away then rinsed the cloth, wrung it out and bathed his face, willing him to open his eyes and recognise her.

But he seemed to be unaware of her presence. She gently straightened the sheet, hesitating to touch the bandage which still encircled his chest. She had changed it that morning, applying the salve the doctor had left.

'There, Pa. I'll come back later to see how you are,' she whispered, picking up the bowl and the cloth.

But at the door, something made her turn back. Perhaps she should have a look at the wound, check if the inflammation was starting to go down. She put the bowl down and pulled back the sheet, undoing the bandage with trembling fingers. As she pulled it away, the smell told her that something was badly wrong. She hardly dared look.

Covering her mouth with her hand she rushed outside, gulping in the fresh air. 'Oh, Pa, what shall I do?' she muttered, clutching the door jamb for support. She must go back in, do what she could for her poor father. But first she must get someone to go for the doctor.

She looked across the green towards the post office and the inn but there was no sign of life. The village slumbered peacefully in the noon sunshine. Where was everybody?

She took a couple of frantic steps towards the inn, gasping with relief when she saw a small boy bowling his hoop along the dusty track. 'Hey, boy — young Billy, isn't it?' she called. 'Would you like to earn a penny?'

The boy nodded eagerly.

'Run to Doctor Tate's — tell him to come to the smithy. Tell him it's urgent, please.'

'Where's my penny then?'

'You'll get it when you've fetched the doctor,' Tilly said.

The boy grinned and ran off, leaving his hoop spinning on the ground outside the cottage. Tilly sighed with relief. He'd do the errand all right and be back for his hoop as well as his penny.

She went back indoors and bathed her father's face again. Was he worse? Where was Doctor Tate? Why didn't he come? Reluctant as she was to leave Ben, she ran outside again, peering down the lane and listening for the sound of his car.

She was about to turn away when young Billy appeared, hot and out of breath. 'Did you tell him? Where is he?' Tilly grabbed the boy's arm and shook him roughly.

'He's on his rounds, the lady said. She'll tell him when he gets back.' Billy pulled away, rubbing his arm. 'Where's my penny, then?'

Tilly felt ashamed. It wasn't the lad's fault. She went indoors and returned with a penny and a halfpenny.

'Cor, thanks, miss.' Billy grabbed his hoop and ran off down the lane, leaving Tilly to pace up and down, alternately peering up the lane and going indoors to check on her father.

At last she heard the noisy car engine and the doctor's vehicle bumped up the lane, coming to a halt in the smithy yard.

'What's amiss then? I told you there wasn't anything else I could do — it was just a matter of letting the wound heal,' Doctor Tate said, grabbing his bag and striding towards her.

'It's not healing, doctor. And he seems much worse today.' Tilly led him into the parlour.

Doctor Tate leaned over the bed and pulled back the sheet, drawing in his breath as the smell reached his nostrils.

He did not have to say anything. Tilly had known from the moment she unwrapped the bandage that things were bad and she could tell from the doctor's expression that he agreed.

He removed the bandage and tenderly probed the wound, pressing his fingers into the surrounding puffy flesh. Then he replaced both the bandage and the sheet and straightened up, gesturing silently for Tilly to follow him into the other room.

'I'm so sorry, Miss Masters. We've done all we can.' He shook his head.

'Is it . . . ?' She could not say the word.

'Gangrene.' He nodded. 'If it were an arm or a leg we could amputate and there would be some hope but . . . '

Tilly choked back a sob. 'Is there

nothing you can do?'

'I'm sorry. Just keep him as comfortable as possible.'

★   ★   ★

Ben lingered for two more days and Tilly did not leave his side. Word soon spread round the village that the blacksmith was dying and his former customers dropped by with gifts of food and words of comfort. But Tilly was scarcely aware of the comings and goings. Even when Ben had drawn his last breath, she stayed by his side, holding his hand, reluctant to leave.

'You must rest, love.' A hand on her shoulder made her look up and she realised it was Aunt Ada. How long had she been here?

'I can't leave him,' Tilly said, shaking her head as the tears welled up.

Ada's hand was firm on her shoulder. 'You must, dear. There's nothing you can do now. He's gone; he's at peace.' She helped Tilly to her feet and led her into the kitchen.

Two village women were there —
Rose and Edith — friends of her
mother, people she had known since
childhood. They offered their condo-
lences and promised to do all that was
necessary.

'Leave everything to us, love,' Edith
said.

'That's right, Tilly. You go up and
have a nice sleep. You look exhausted.'
Rose patted her arm. 'Go along with
you.'

Tilly managed a tearful smile of
thanks and dragged herself up the
narrow stair. She looked round the little
room as if she were a stranger there,
so unfamiliar did it seem after weeks of
sleeping downstairs to keep an eye on
her father. A sob escaped her and she
threw herself down on the narrow bed
and gave herself up to her grief and
despair.

8

Tilly had been staying with her aunt since the funeral. Although she didn't really want to leave the forge untended, she had reluctantly given in to Ada's repeated pleas.

'You can't stay here alone, girl,' she'd said.

Why not? Tilly thought. She had been managing alone since her father's illness. But at last she'd been forced to admit that it would be hard to carry on as usual. Business had fallen off. Caring for Ben had left her little time to make new horseshoes and to carry out the urgent equipment repairs that were needed at harvest time, this most busy period of the year. She could not blame the farmers for going further afield to get the jobs done.

If only Ben had recovered, or if Nathan had survived the war, Tilly was sure that between them they would have been able to rebuild the business. But it was not to be.

With a heavy heart she had closed up the cottage and the smithy, but she could not bring herself to sell her father's tools, or let the cottage to someone else. She didn't say so, but she had no intention of staying with her aunt forever.

It was true that she needed a rest after the weeks of nursing her father, but as she locked the cottage door for the last time, she told herself that she'd be back one day.

Famer Johnson had agreed to keep an eye on the place for her but she could tell he thought her foolish for not selling up completely and making a new life for herself.

A new life, she thought, as she sat in her aunt's parlour, trying in vain to turn a heel on the sock she was knitting. Her hands, so deft with the blacksmith's tools, seemed incapable of obeying her when it came to knitting and sewing.

She sat up straighter, determined to master this skill as she had others in her short life. *If only I could take pride in it,* she thought. *If it were for Nathan, I'd do it,* she told herself. *So why not for those other young lads still out there, fighting for King and country?* This dreadful war still dragged on and there seemed to be no end in sight, despite the optimistic headlines in the daily papers, which Aunt Ada read out each morning at breakfast.

Her depressing thoughts were interrupted by a knock on the parlour door and she looked up, expecting to see Dora, the maid. But it was her aunt.

'Mr Lacey is here,' Ada announced with a self-satisfied smile, stepping back to allow Richard to enter.

He had called frequently since she had come to stay in town and Aunt Ada had encouraged her to be nice to him, hinting that he was more than interested in her.

Tilly could not deny that he was handsome as well as being good company, and his visits broke the monotony of her life in Lydmouth. But she just could not imagine feeling about him the way she had about Nathan and she certainly didn't care about his social position or his wealth.

Tilly felt a little lurch in her stomach as she put down her knitting and greeted him warily. He took her hand and kissed it before sitting beside her on the sofa. Her aunt smiled and closed the door, leaving them together.

Tilly tried to rise. She didn't want to be alone with him. Besides, he might take her enjoyment of his company for encouragement. 'I'll fetch refreshments,' she said. 'I'm sure you'd like a cooling drink after your ride.'

'Your aunt is seeing to it,' he said, laying a hand on her arm. 'Sit down, Tilly. I want to talk to you.'

Her heart began to beat faster. She thought she knew what he was going to say. Aunt Ada had hinted that he was sure to propose before long. How would she answer him? She had always said she would only marry for love, as her own parents had done. But her one true love was gone. Her life now was empty, and all she could see in the future were even more long empty days. Living in town and catering to her aunt's whims, becoming a lonely spinster doing 'good works', was not the life she had imagined for herself.

She thought back to those carefree days in the forge at Lydford. Yes, the work was hard. But there was the satisfaction of a job well done, an outlet for her creative, artistic spirit. She would never know that again, living the life her aunt wanted for her. But as Richard's wife, would things be any different? As mistress of Lynton Manor she would have to live by a different set of rules, just as stifling to her carefree nature.

She sat twisting her hands in her lap, scarcely taking in what Richard was saying. She would never forget Nathan, but could she leave her former life behind her forever, give herself to Richard, knowing she would never love him in the same way? She did like him — but was that really enough?

As she opened her mouth to say so, he stopped speaking and leaned towards her, taking her hands in his. 'Answer me, Tilly. Tell me you'll say yes. I'm sure you feel something for me. And I love you. I promise I'll take care of you; you'll never want for anything . . . '

Tilly tried to pull her hands away from him. 'Richard, please, I don't know what to say.'

He pulled her towards him, clasping her hands to his chest. 'Just say 'yes'.' He began to kiss her, his lips travelling over her cheeks, her eyelids and lastly to her mouth. She tried to push him away but his grasp tightened as his tongue probed her lips.

She managed to pull herself free and took a deep breath. 'Richard, please, let me think.'

'There's nothing to think about. I love you, I need you . . . '

'But Richard, I can't marry you. I don't love you.'

His eyes widened and he gasped. 'You can't . . . ?' He began to laugh. 'Marry? Who said anything about marriage? Have you lost your senses, girl? How can I marry you? My father would cut me off in a wink. I'd lose absolutely everything.'

Tilly stared at him, her eyes blazing in her chalk white face.

Before she could speak, his laughter turned to a snort of disbelief and he pushed her away. 'You stupid girl. Did you really think I meant marriage? To you, the blacksmith's daughter?'

He stood up and stalked across the room, throwing open the door just as Ada returned carrying a loaded tray.

'Are you leaving so soon?' she asked, bewilderment on her face as Richard pushed past her and rushed out of the house.

'What did you say to him?' she snapped. 'Surely you didn't turn him down, you stupid child.'

Tilly stood up and took a deep breath. 'That's the second time I've been called stupid in the past five minutes,' she said. 'And, yes, I did turn him down. Would you have preferred me to agree to his proposal, then?'

'Why not? He's one of the most eligible men in the district.' Ada put the tray down and faced her niece. 'You would have been set up for life.'

'Yes. Set up as his mistress in a discreet little house tucked away out of sight of respectable society, visited at his whim.'

'I don't understand. I was sure he meant to propose marriage; he hinted as much to me.' Ada felt for a chair and sat down.

Tilly sat down beside her and took her aunt's hand. 'It seems we've both been misled.' She could not say the word 'stupid', although she did now feel rather foolish. Of course a man in Richard Lacey's position would not propose marriage to someone of her station.

She thought back to the new year ball and the stares of the guests as he had danced with her. Had they been speculating as to his interest in her?

But he had been so kind during her father's illness, and she had begun to feel a certain warmth towards him. Now a tide of anger rose in her and she stood up, beginning to pace the room with clenched fists. He had been leading her on, letting her think he truly loved her, while all the time he had been planning to seduce her.

Her aunt seemed to have recovered from the shock and began to pour the tea. 'Sit down, dear. And calm yourself. At least you found out in time what sort of man he is. There will be other opportunities. You are young and pretty and you will have all this when I . . . ' She waved a hand to indicate the house and its substantial furnishings.

'Please don't speak of that, Aunt. I can't think of losing you too. Besides, you know I don't care about material things.' She gave a little half sob, half laugh. 'I thought he loved me.' At that moment it didn't matter that she would have turned him down anyway. The humiliation hurt more.

'Well, he probably does — in his way.'

'But for him to think that I would . . . '

'Be glad you found him out before you did anything silly,' Ada said, patting her hand. 'Put it behind you, dear. Not all men are like that.'

No, they're not, thought Tilly and a memory of Nathan filled her mind, despite her resolve not to dwell on the past.

She pushed her cup away and stood up again. 'I can't stay here,' she choked, and rushed out of the room.

Upstairs she pulled the battered carpet bag down from the top of the wardrobe. *How dare he?* she fumed. Useless to tell herself that even if he'd proposed marriage, she would have turned him down. Furious anger made her heart beat faster and her breath came raggedly as she began to throw things haphazardly into the bag. It was humiliating. Surely everyone in this small harbour town knew of his frequent visits to her aunt's house, would have been speculating as to Richard Lacey's interest in her. Perhaps they thought she was already his mistress?

She threw herself down on the bed, covering her face with her hands, tears seeping between her fingers. *Was this my aunt's doing?* she asked herself, remembering Ada's involvement in organising the ball at the manor, her own hinted hopes of a relationship with Richard's father. But no, Ada was a respectable widow. Surely she too had been misled into thinking that Richard's intentions were honourable.

It didn't matter. Tilly knew she could not stay in Lydmouth where every time she went out she would be conscious of knowing looks and nods, whether imagined or not.

She stood up and began to pack her bag more methodically.

The new gowns her aunt had had made for her could stay behind, she decided. She would have no use for them where she was going. Hanging on a hook at the back of the wardrobe was her leather blacksmith's apron, scarred and scorched by sparks from the fire. Tilly took it down and folded it carefully, held it against her face, inhaling the smell of old leather, imagining it still held the scent of heated iron and glowing coals.

A lump rose in her throat as she remembered those happy carefree days as a child, learning the blacksmith's craft alongside her father — dear, patient, dependable Ben Masters. Then later, when Nathan came to work with them, the forge had rung with the sound of laughter as well as the clang of hammer on iron. She was scarcely aware of it as the friendship and respect she'd had for Nathan gradually grew to a deep and abiding love — a love that would not die and which still clung to the desperate hope that somehow, somewhere he had survived and would be restored to her. *That hope is all I have now,* she thought, as she smoothed the old apron and laid it on top of her few meagre possessions.

She fastened the bag and moved towards the door, pausing to take one last look round the room which her aunt had furnished specially for her — the pretty frilled counterpane and matching curtains, the rose-sprigged china jug and basin on the washstand. Pretty and welcoming as it was, though, it wasn't home and never would be.

She slowly descended the stairs, swallowing painfully as she tried to decide what to say to her aunt.

Ada was standing in the hall, her lips tight, her hands clasped in front of her. 'You don't have to go, Tilly. What will you do? How will you live?'

'You know I can't stay here, Aunt,' she said, a sob catching in her throat.

'I don't see why not. No one need know what happened here today and I'm sure Mr Lacey will keep quiet about it. After all, he will not wish to share his own humiliation.'

'His humiliation? What about mine?'
Anger flared again in Tilly's breast. 'I
still cannot believe he would insult me
so.' She put the bag down and took a
deep breath. 'It's not your fault, Aunt.
We have both been duped. But I can't
stay.' She moved towards the older
woman and put her arms around her in
an awkward hug. 'Thank you for
everything you've done for me. I'm so
sorry things didn't work out in the way
you wanted.'

'I'm sorry too, my dear.' Ada patted
Tilly's back before letting her go. 'I
suppose you're going back to the
smithy to take up your father's reins.
Well, I suppose I can't stop you.' She
gave a wry smile. 'Just like your mother,
headstrong, knowing your own mind.'

Tilly opened the front door and
picked up the battered bag. 'If I hurry I
believe I'll be able to pick up the
carrier's cart at the end of the road.'

As she quickly walked away, Ada
called out to her. 'Don't forget — I'm
still here if you need anything.'

Tilly looked back and smiled. 'I won't forget.' Then she quickly turned the corner, anxious to put Lydmouth and the past few weeks behind her as soon as possible. Her old life beckoned. *No, not the old one,* she told herself. It was a new life ahead of her — no longer the blacksmith's daughter but Tilly Masters, the village blacksmith.

9

Dusk was falling and the autumn day had turned chilly as Tilly jumped down from the carrier's cart and crossed the village green to the smithy. She opened the cottage door, shivering as she entered the kitchen and frowning at the accumulated dust on the shelves and furniture.

She lit the lamp and set to, riddling the ashes from the bottom of the range and lighting the fire. She pumped water into the big cast iron kettle and set it on the hob. She'd have to get up early tomorrow and give the place a good clean, she thought.

Reluctantly, she opened the parlour door. Her father's bed was still there, the sofa pushed to one side, and Tilly swallowed a lump in her throat, remembering the nights she had spent there tending to him in his last days.

She closed the door hurriedly and, picking up the lamp, she crossed the yard to the forge.

Everything was as she had left it — was it only weeks ago? As in the cottage, a fine film of dust clung to everything, an air of neglect and disuse. But there was coal in the bin, stacks of bar iron waiting to be forged and tools arrayed ready for use.

On the bench in the corner, she noticed the gate latch that Richard Lacey had left for her to repair. She picked it up, tempted to throw it across the yard. But practicality won and she put in on the heap of scrap iron. Her father had never thrown anything away if it could be re-used. Even the tiniest piece of scrap iron could be melted down and made into something useful. Too bad if Richard Lacey turned up expecting the latch to be repaired. *Serve him right,* she thought.

It was too dark now to think of starting work and she returned to the cottage. The water was hot now and she used some of it to wash the dust off the crockery arrayed on the dresser. Then she made herself a drink and sat down at the table, her head in her hands.

Had she done the right thing, leaving the comfort of her aunt's home and coming back here? Could she start up the forge again and make a living? She only knew she had to try. Overcome with emotion and exhaustion, she dragged herself up the stairs and, without bothering to undress, she threw herself down on the bed.

Before extinguishing the lamp, she looked round the familiar little room and smiled. *I'm home,* she thought, and closed her eyes.

To her surprise, she slept well and woke to sunshine streaming in at the window. Firmly pushing the events of the day before to the back of her mind, she washed and changed into her working dress, found some oatmeal in the bin in the larder and made some porridge. She'd have to stock up on provisions at the village shop, but first she must put the cottage in order.

Three hours later every surface was gleaming, the table scrubbed, the floor swept, mats beaten free of dust. Tilly stood in the doorway and nodded with satisfaction. She smoothed her dress and tidied her hair and strolled across the green to the shop.

It took her longer than she'd anticipated as people greeted her and welcomed her back. 'Thought you were staying with your aunt for good,' Miss Lillywhite, the postmistress, said.

'I changed my mind,' said Tilly.

'You're surely not going to set up on your own.' Miss Lillywhite gave a sniff of disapproval. 'You'll need a man to help.'

'I'm sure I'll manage,' Tilly answered.

It was the same when she went into the store. Although most of the villagers had begun to accept her as her father's assistant, especially when Nathan went away, they found it hard to accept the idea of a young girl running the smithy on her own.

I'll show them, she thought, as she returned to the cottage with her basket of provisions. She put the groceries away and went across to the smithy. Time to fire up the forge and start work.

With no customers yet, she decided to shape some of the bar iron into horse shoes. There was always the chance of a famer needing his horse shod in a hurry. When passers-by heard the sound of hammer on iron, they would realise the forge was in action again. The word would soon get round and she was sure she'd be able to make a passable living.

A stack of heavy carthorse shoes was finished and Tilly wiped her forehead with an old rag. Looking round for something else to do, her eye fell on Richard Lacey's broken gate latch which still rested on top of the heap of scrap iron. *Might as well mend it,* she thought.

She spread more coal on the forge bed and waited for it to start glowing.

When she'd done the job, she would ask the carrier to deliver it to Lynton Manor. She hoped she'd never see Richard Lacey again.

★　★　★

Nathan opened his eyes, squinting against the late autumn sun which slanted through a crack in the barn wall. Today, all was quiet and once again he dared to hope that the war was almost over and at last he could go home. But, as he struggled to his feet and limped across to the doorway, the barrage started up again, louder than ever.

It was hard to tell which side it was; the lines had ebbed and flowed across this stretch of ruined farmland for the past few months.

Once, when he was still delirious with pain, he thought he had heard English voices close by. He had hauled himself up, calling out, 'Ginge, over here, mate,' thinking his old mate had

159

come to rescue him.

But his voice was a feeble croak and the voices faded away as he drifted out of consciousness again. When he woke again, he told himself it had just been a dream. Ginger was dead, Captain Weston probably was, too — and that lovely horse. He had shed more tears over the horses than he had over his companions. They'd had no choice, whereas he, and hundreds like him, had volunteered for this nightmare.

The thoughts churned round in his head as he listened to the distant guns, wondering at the luck which had brought him to this lonely farmhouse. He could scarcely remember pulling himself out of the shell hole and crawling across no man's land towards the wire. He didn't want to leave Captain Weston, but he had to get help.

It was only as he was about to struggle to his feet and call out that he heard the guttural tones of the sentry and realised that, in the darkness, he had been crawling in the wrong direction. He scuttled away as fast as his wounded leg would allow until he reached a small copse, the trees shattered by repeated shelling. But enough remained to give him shelter.

Exhausted, he had burrowed into a pile of dead leaves and let himself sleep at last.

He was woken by someone shaking his shoulder and he started up, only to have a rough hand clamped over his mouth. A hoarse voice whispered something in French and he shook his head, looking up into the wrinkled face of an old woman. She smiled, revealing a gap in her teeth, took her hand away from his mouth, and beckoned to him.

'You come?' she said. She mimed eating with her hand, nodding and smiling. 'Vous avez faim?' she asked.

She seemed to be asking if he was hungry and, although he didn't understand her words, he nodded.

She held out her hand and helped him to his feet. He staggered as pain shot through his wounded leg and she picked up a branch and handed it to him. Leaning heavily on it, he followed the old woman through the copse and alongside a stream.

Was she helping him or was she going to hand him over as a prisoner? At this moment he didn't care. At least he'd be fed in a prison camp.

He smiled now, remembering how suspicious he had been of Marie. Over the past months she had been his only human contact. She had insisted he slept in the barn, hiding under bales of straw when German patrols came near. But she allowed him into her dilapidated farmhouse for his meals — simple fare of bread and eggs, vegetables from the garden.

As winter turned to spring and spring to summer, Nathan had picked up a few words of French and had learned that Marie's husband had been shot, her two sons sent to a labour camp. Why the Germans had spared her she couldn't tell — unless it was because she had managed to keep the little farm going and supplied them with eggs and fresh vegetables.

As soon as his strength returned, Nathan had repaid her kindness by helping in the garden and making small repairs around the farm. He couldn't do too much for fear of arousing suspicion when the German patrols dropped by to pick up their provisions.

Nathan sighed as he stood at the barn door, breathing in the smoky air. Winter would soon be upon them and still there was no end to the war. Would he ever get home to his sweetheart? Determinedly thrusting thoughts of Tilly behind him, he limped across the farmyard and began to haul buckets of water up from the well.

Marie came out of the house and, instead of beginning to feed the chickens as she usually did, she hobbled towards him, smiling her toothless smile and waving her hands around as she did when she was excited.

He smiled and called out, 'Bonjour, Marie.'

She took a deep breath as she approached, 'Rene has just come from the village — he has news. La guerre, Nathan — la guerre est finie.'

He stared at her blankly, unable to take in the words, his meagre French deserting him. 'La guerre — the war?'

She nodded, grinning. 'Oui, Oui, finie.'

'Finished?' He could scarcely believe it. 'But the guns? I heard them.' As he spoke he realised that the guns had been silent for some time. A huge grin spread over his face and he put the bucket down, grabbing Marie's hands and whirling her round the yard. 'Is it really over — I can go home?'

She pushed him away, holding her hand over her chest and laughing. Then the smile faded. 'You will go, Nathan? Back to your Tilly?'

He nodded. 'But not just yet, Marie. We must make sure it is safe — for you too. And I'll help you harvest the potatoes before I go.'

They stood in the quiet of the

farmyard, only the clucking of the hens breaking the silence, trying to take in what the news meant.

Faintly, on the still frosty air, came the sound of church bells ringing.

★ ★ ★

Hopes were high that the end of the war was in sight but now the newspaper headlines were dominated by the epidemic of Spanish flu which had devastated much of Europe and had now reached England. In the towns hundreds of people had already died.

Here in the quiet countryside it did not seem to affect them so much but when Tilly heard from the weekly carrier that it had reached Lydmouth, she began to worry about her aunt.

She had scarcely given Ada a thought since returning to the village. Word had spread that she was back and trying to manage the forge on her own and several of Ben's former customers had turned up with jobs for her. A few were dubious about her ability to rebuild the business but some, like Farmer Johnson, were prepared to give her a chance.

She was barely scraping a living, but it was enough for her. At last resigned to spending the rest of her life alone, she was finding a small measure of contentment in doing the work she loved. Her one regret was that she would have no son or daughter to follow in her footsteps.

Her content was shattered one day in early November when she received a note from her aunt's maid saying that Ada was very ill with the influenza and was asking for her. Once more she closed up the forge and the cottage and crossed the village green to wait for the carrier's cart.

For three days Aunt Ada hovered on the brink of death while Tilly never left her side. As she tenderly bathed the older woman's forehead and tried to get her to sip cooling lemonade, she regretted bitterly how often she had resented Ada's criticism of her chosen career and her impatience with the interference in her life.

Her mother's sister was now her only living relative. If she died, Tilly would have no one. As she sat at the bedside, holding her aunt's hand, she choked back her sobs, praying that she would be spared.

Suddenly the bedroom door was flung open and Dora, Ada's excitable maid, stood there, her face alight. 'Listen, miss — listen — the bells.'

'Shh, Dora, don't disturb your mistress. What's happened?'

'Can't you hear them? — they're ringing the bells. The war's over!'

For a moment Tilly couldn't take it in. Her life had been so bound up in nursing her aunt that the war news had faded into the background. She stood up and ushered the girl out of the room, glancing behind her to where Aunt Ada slept.

Outside on the landing she gripped Dora's arm. 'Is it really over?'

'The butcher's boy just told me, then the bells started to peal so I knew it was true.' Dora started to cry. 'I can't believe it, we've prayed for so long. I'm happy but sad too — all those boys who won't be coming home, my brother, my cousin . . .'

Tilly tried to swallow the lump in her own throat. 'Nathan, why did you have to go?' she muttered. Squaring her shoulders, she patted Dora's arm. 'At least it's all over now — don't cry, Dora. Go and make us a nice cup of tea. I'll just make sure Aunt's all right and then I'll come and join you.'

Ada appeared to be sleeping peacefully now. Tilly felt her forehead and was relieved to find that the fever seemed to be abating. She would be all right for a while.

She went downstairs to find Dora standing by the area door, a fixed smile on her plump face. 'Listen, miss,' she said as Tilly went to join her.

Over the sound of the church bells they could hear a roaring noise, like a stormy sea, coming from the direction of the town square. Tilly realised the sound was a swell of excited voices, some singing, some shouting as the news was passed from one to another.

Dora turned to Tilly and asked her pleadingly, 'Can I go, miss? All my friends will be celebrating.'

'Go on then.' Tilly smiled as the girl tore off her apron and grabbed a coat from the back of the door. As she raced up the area steps and disappeared in the direction of the harbour, Tilly's smile faded. She had nothing to celebrate.

Slowly, she went inside and climbed the stairs to her aunt's room. The shades were partly drawn and, in the gloom, she could just make out Ada's still figure. She gasped and hurried over to the bed. How could she have left her, even for a minute?

Tentatively, she stretched out a hand to touch her aunt's face, starting back as her eyes opened.

'Tilly, what are you doing here?'

Ada's voice was weak.

Half laughing, half crying, Tilly stroked the damp hair back from the older woman's brow. 'You're better,' she said. 'Oh, Aunt, you've been so ill. I thought . . . ' She choked back a sob.

'Nonsense, I'm never ill.' Ada struggled to sit up, but the effort was too much for her. Gasping, she fell back against the pillows. 'I must admit, I do feel a bit peculiar. I felt a bit giddy and Dora insisted I went to bed.' She plucked at the sheet. 'She shouldn't have sent for you though. I just needed a rest, that's all.'

'Aunt, believe me, you have been ill. I've been here for three days but Dora was nursing you before that. The doctor insisted she sent for me.'

'I don't need a doctor . . . ' Ada's voice trailed away and her eyes closed. Within seconds, she was sleeping, but this time it was deep healing sleep.

Tilly bathed her face and straightened the sheets, then tiptoed away. Downstairs in the basement kitchen, she sat at the table, while outside, the bells continued their clamour and now and then she heard footsteps running, bright voices calling the news out to each other.

The war was over, Aunt Ada wasn't going to die, and life could go back to normal. But Nathan and hundreds of others wouldn't be coming home. Overcome by exhaustion and the turrnoil of emotions, Tilly's head dropped into her hands and she, too, slept.

*　*　*

The armistice had been signed but, for many of those who had survived, it would be weeks or even months before they saw their homes again. Nathan knew that he would have to make his own way back to the coast through the wasteland that had been left behind by four years of conflict.

Although he was impatient to be gone, he was determined to fulfil his promise to Marie and help her with the potato harvest. It was the least he could do after her care of him. And, now that he was free of the fear of discovery, he was able to move about freely and do so much more of the farm work. Rusting farm implements and broken machinery kept him busy in those first weeks after the bells had rung out from the village church.

In all that time he did not stop thinking of Tilly and dreaming of their reunion. He hoped it wasn't just a dream. Common sense told him that she must think him dead. And if that were so, would she have given in to Ada Bradford's badgering and left the forge? Could she have met someone else? Was it asking too much that she should be true to his memory — at least for a while, long enough for him to get home and declare his love?

He thrust the gloomy thoughts away and straightened his back as he patted down the last clamp of potatoes, a good store against the coming winter. He summoned a smile as Marie hobbled towards him, her mouth wide in a toothless grin. 'Les pommes de terre — the potatoes — are . . . ' She waved her hands trying to think of the right word.

'Yes, all done.'

'Merci.' She patted his arm. 'You will wish to be gone now?'

'Well . . . ' He hesitated. Yes, he was anxious to get away but guilt smote him as he recalled her kindness.

'You must go,' she said. 'You cannot spend your life here with an old woman. You must go back to your Tilly, non?'

'I'll leave in the morning,' he said, trying hard to disguise his relief.

★   ★   ★

Once the fever had broken, Ada began to recover, although she remained weak for several weeks. Tilly longed to get back to the forge and what she thought of as her real life, but even now she couldn't leave until she was sure that her aunt would not suffer a relapse. The doctor had warned her that this type of influenza sometimes had lasting effects, weakening the constitution, so that the slightest thing could cause a setback in her recovery.

'Her heart is not strong and a winter chill could be the finish of her,' the doctor had said.

'Don't worry, I'll look after her,' Tilly assured him.

As Ada's strength returned so too did her old bossy ways. Before long, she was ordering Tilly and Dora around, and making plans for elaborate Christmas celebrations.

'It is a real cause for celebration this year,' she said. 'After all, I missed out on the singing and dancing when the war ended. After four years of gloom, we need cheering up. We'll have a dinner party.'

Tilly had to point out that many of her aunt's acquaintances would not be celebrating. Everyone in town had lost somebody to the war and now the influenza was sweeping the country and taking more with it. But she couldn't dampen Ada's enthusiasm.

'We'll have a New Year party then. I'll be back to normal by then,' she said. 'Write this down, Tilly.'

From her place on the chaise longue in the drawing room, Ada dictated a guest list, shopping lists for food and decorations.

Tilly was thrown back on recollections of the previous year when she had helped to organise the new year charity ball and Richard Lacey had begun to take notice of her.

So much had happened since then and yet, here she was back where she had started. She had not dreamed she would still be at her aunt's beck and call, while back in Lydford the forge lay dusty and unattended, the fire forever cold.

No, not forever, Tilly thought rebelliously, throwing down the latest list and declaring that she needed some fresh air. She went outside into the cold, frosty garden. Ada was well again now, she didn't need her any more, she thought, as she paced the paths between the empty flower beds. Yes, she would do her duty and stay till after the dinner party. But then she would go back to Lydford, back to where her heart lay.

10

Nathan got off the train and stood for a moment looking around him at the familiar sights, the cobbled road leading down to the town square and, beyond it, the harbour where he had embarked for France so long ago.

Still limping slightly, he walked up the street leading out of town towards Wendon. Desperate as he was to see Tilly, his duty was to his mother. He had written to Tilly from Dover telling her of his miraculous rescue and the long trek across the unfamiliar French countryside.

After making sure his mother was all right, he would catch a ride on a carrier's cart and hasten to Lydford. Anticipation of their reunion quickened his steps. He passed the end of the road leading to Ada Bradford's house and wondered if he should call and seek news of Tilly. After a momentary hesitation he walked on. Ada Bradford had never had time for him, thinking a lowly blacksmith wasn't good enough for her niece. Tilly had told him that her aunt had never forgiven her sister for marrying beneath her.

★ ★ ★

After spending two days with his mother, eating until he could eat no more, enjoying the nights between clean white sheets, the warmth of the kitchen range, he gently told her that he had to be off.

She looked at him through misty eyes. 'Tis good to have you back, Nathan lad. But I know where your heart lies.'

Nathan felt himself reddening under gaze. 'It's not just that, Mother,' he protested. 'I have to earn a living now. God knows how you've been managing since the army stopped my allowance.' He held up a hand. 'I know you've been taking in washing, but there's no need now. I know Ben Masters will take me back and now that I'm a Master Sergeant Farrier — 'he threw out his chest in mock pride — 'I'll be earning a good living.'

The grin faded as he saw her expression. 'What is it, Mother?'

Mrs Miller shook her head. 'Oh, son. Of course, you can't have known. I should have told you straight away. I'm sorry, lad. Ben Masters died — back in the summer.'

Nathan sat down heavily. 'Ben, dead? What happened to the forge — and to Tilly?'

'I believe she tried to keep going. But last I heard she was living with her aunt in town.'

'Tilly's in Lydmouth? She's left the forge?' Why hadn't he obeyed his impulse and called at Mrs Bradford's? He and Tilly could have been together already by now.

His mother touched his arm gently. 'I did hear that Ada Bradford has ambitions for her niece. I know you hoped . . . ' Her voice trailed away.

Nathan shook his head and groaned. So, it looked as if she had done as her aunt wanted after all.

His mother was looking worried. 'What will you do, son?'

'Who's taken over the forge?' he asked.

'No one, as far as I've heard. It's standing empty.'

'I'll have to find out who owns it now. But the village needs a smith and a farrier. Maybe I can take it over.'

* * *

Tilly had walked the three miles from Lydmouth and her feet were sore, but her heart lifted as she looked across the village green towards the smithy. It had been hard to leave her aunt without a pang of guilt. She felt in her pocket for Ada's parting gift and smiled. As she said goodbye, her aunt had pressed the little jar into her hand and said, 'Don't forget to use it regularly, my dear. Marigold and lavender. It'll keep those hands soft and help any little cuts to heal more quickly.'

Yes, no doubt she meant well but she was well on the way to recovery now and would no doubt soon be back to her usual bossy ways. Tilly was sure she would be all right and Dora had promised to send a message if she should suffer a relapse. Besides, she couldn't go on living on her aunt's charity. It was time she got back to work.

As she neared the old thatched building she saw a wisp of smoke drifting across the roof. She started to run. The building must be on fire. What had caused it? Village boys playing around?

But as she got closer she heard the ring of hammer on iron and the sound of cheerful whistling. She stopped, her hand to her mouth, her heart hammering. No, it couldn't be. She was dreaming. She took a few hesitant steps towards the smithy, peering into the gloom. The forge was glowing and a figure stood there, his back bent over the bar as he twisted it into shape. She stopped.

The man was thin, his clothes hung on him like a scarecrow. No, this couldn't be Nathan, the bonny, brawny lad who had left her so long ago. A burst of anger coursed through her. How dare someone come in and take over her livelihood without a by your leave? She stepped towards the stranger, hot words on her lips.

He straightened and turned round, a smile lighting up his gaunt features.

'Nathan?' she whispered.

'Tilly! You're here. I thought . . . '

She rushed towards him, arms outstretched, a sob bursting from her throat. 'Why didn't you tell me you were home? I would have been here.'

He took her in his arms, holding her as if he would never let go. 'I wrote. Didn't you get my letter?' He pushed her gently away, gazing into her eyes. 'It doesn't matter, you're here now.'

Tilly's eyes filled and the tears she had repressed for so long overflowed. But this time they were tears of happiness. 'They told me you were dead but I never really gave up hope.'

Gently, Nathan wiped away her tears with his thumb. 'It was the thought of you that kept me going. Sometimes I thought I'd never get home.'

'The war's been over for months. What happened to you?'

'It's a long story — too long to go into now. I'll tell you one day, but at this moment, I have more important things on my mind.'

Tilly smiled and a mischievous dimple appeared. 'Like that bar iron that's overheated?' she asked, gesturing towards the forge, where sparks were beginning to fly up towards the ceiling.

'Much more important than that,' he said as he pulled her into his arms and kissed her as she'd never been kissed before.

We do hope that you have enjoyed reading this large print book.

Did you know that all of our titles are available for purchase?

We publish a wide range of high quality large print books including:
Romances, Mysteries, Classics
General Fiction
Non Fiction and Westerns

Special interest titles available in large print are:
The Little Oxford Dictionary
Music Book, Song Book
Hymn Book, Service Book

Also available from us courtesy of Oxford University Press:
Young Readers' Dictionary
(large print edition)
Young Readers' Thesaurus
(large print edition)

For further information or a free brochure, please contact us at:
Ulverscroft Large Print Books Ltd.,
The Green, Bradgate Road, Anstey,
Leicester, LE7 7FU, England.
Tel: (00 44) **0116 236 4325**
Fax: (00 44) **0116 234 0205**

JUST IN TIME FOR CHRISTMAS

Moyra Tarling

Vienna was just a girl when she came to live with Tobias Sheridan and his son, Drew. But when a bitter family feud sent Drew packing, he'd left town, unaware of Vienna's secret passion for him . . . Now he was back. A widower, Drew had returned for the holidays with the grandson his father had never known. But when he took the lovely, grown-up Vienna in his arms, he knew he'd come home at last — just in time for Christmas.

Please return / renew by date shown.
You can renew it at:
norlink.norfolk.gov.uk
or by telephone: 0344 800 8006
Please have your library card & PIN ready

26/03/13
18/4/13
08. OCT 15
8MN

28. JUN 24